Sherazad had slept in his arms.

She'd let him hug her all night and shared the comforts of her generous spirit and warm body with him.

Now Lorenzo didn't dare shift one aching muscle. She'd wake up if he did. Then she'd move away. He couldn't bear that.

Just one more hour like this. He needed just one more hour. Then he'd let her go. Once he did, he'd never hold her again.

The next second she opened her eyes. And looked directly into his soul.

No! He *needed* his one more hour.

But if he couldn't have it, he'd have one more kiss.

Dear Reader,

It's always easy to lose perspective, to think that one's own plight is the worst life has to offer. Self-pity can take over, souring your life, sometimes forever.

Refusal to succumb to self-pity drives my heroine Sherazad to the frontline, to remind herself that countless people around the world are suffering far worse than she. Once there, she meets my hero Lorenzo in a genuinely worst-case situation! It's only the beginning of a series of adventures that heal Sherazad's scars, awaken her heart and restore her faith in herself and the human race, as she learns to focus not on those who thrive on cruelty, but those who give their very lives for others.

In this, my first published book, it was a true pleasure to explore the journey of self-healing and sacrifice that Lorenzo and Sherazad embark on only to end up finding the ultimate reward: true love.

I hope you enjoy their journey, too.

Olivia Gates

Doctors on the Frontline

Olivia Gates

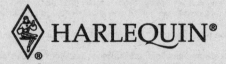

HARLEQUIN®

TORONTO • NEW YORK • LONDON
AMSTERDAM • PARIS • SYDNEY • HAMBURG
STOCKHOLM • ATHENS • TOKYO • MILAN • MADRID
PRAGUE • WARSAW • BUDAPEST • AUCKLAND

ISBN 0-373-06469-1

DOCTORS ON THE FRONTLINE

First North American Publication 2004

www.eHarlequin.com

Printed in U.S.A.

CHAPTER ONE

IT WAS another nightmare.

But so what? Sherazad Dawson was used to nightmares. Even if those with Jack in starring roles seemed like pleasant dreams in comparison to this.

This horror movie of a nightmare was understandable, though. She'd been so primed for danger, crossing the war-torn Balkan land, so uncomfortable dozing in the truck, her mind must have had a field day, inventing fantastic terrors.

But why was it so hard to wake up now? At the end of a nightmare she usually shot up wide awake and trembling in fury. Now her eyes felt sealed shut. Her ears roared and her jaw—the man in her nightmare had slammed his fist into it! Surely it wasn't throbbing with an imaginary blow?

And what was that heavy burden pinning her legs down?

Then the foggy sensations receded gradually to uncover one certainty. She *was* pinned flat on her back. Half-crushed beneath a huge body.

Her eyes flew open.

The masked man! From her nightmare!

It was him, half-sprawled over her. It had all been real. *Real.*

The attack on her convoy, her guard and driver shot down, that man streaking towards her truck, trying to enter it…

She'd known she'd die once he did and had decided to die fighting. She'd slammed the door in his face, attacked him tooth and nail. He'd shoved her to the ground, over her dead driver's gun. She'd grabbed it, swung around and just…shot him. He'd staggered and fallen. Then snapped back on his feet. Like a monster from an urban legend who

5

wouldn't stay down. He'd kicked the gun away, nearly her hand with it, picked her up like a rag doll and thrown her back into the truck. She'd still fought like a demented animal. Until he'd knocked her senseless.

It had all happened.

She was really lying beneath him and he was—he was—*dead*!

Thank God.

Now she had to get him off her, find a way out. But she had to breathe first, stop shaking. And when she finally did, she felt it. A movement not originating from her numb body.

His breathing.

He wasn't dead.

A tidal wave of rage, disgust and terror crashed on her. Long paralysed moments later, still choking with dread, she reiterated to herself, *Calm down. Think. Think!*

He wasn't dead, but he *was* out cold. He wasn't a threat—immediately, at least. She had the upper hand for now. She was sore and stiff, with a throbbing and—she knew all too well—multicoloured jaw, but she had no other injuries.

She propped herself on her elbows and looked outside. They were between two mountains, in a narrow ravine that seemed to go on for ever. There was no sign of life of any sort. How had they got here? They'd been nowhere near mountains when his gang had attacked her medical convoy. There was only one answer. Shot and disoriented, he must have driven the truck aimlessly. Until he'd got them lost…

Suddenly, another sensation distracted her from her mounting panic. A sticky heat seeping through her clothes. His blood.

He might still be alive, but he wouldn't be for long if she didn't stop his haemorrhage and…

And why should she? a nasty inner voice asked. Wasn't this the same man she'd been relieved to think dead seconds ago?

No! It was one thing if he was already dead, and another

to *let* him die. She was a doctor. She'd sworn to help anyone who was injured and helpless. Even an enemy.

The voice taunted that if she let him slip away in peace, he'd be the lucky one. With certain death awaiting them in this pitiless terrain, at least *he'd* go quickly.

But I'm still alive, she defied that doomsaying voice. And she intended to *stay* alive. And keep him alive too.

But she had to move fast. Every minute in this cold, even inside the truck, was a sure step towards hypothermia and death.

She started to wriggle, inching her way from beneath him, holding her breath, expecting him to revive at any moment and bear down on her. But he lay as limp as a rag. Or a ton of bricks, more like. Just how much *did* he weigh? No muscle tone made him even heavier. And where were her legs? She could hardly feel them.

A few inches' freedom brought his head rolling against her most intimate place. Nausea filled her up to her eyes. Swearing under her breath, she gave one last shove and sat up, letting him fall face down on the seat.

She jumped out of the truck and bolted away as if from a widening abyss filled with scorpions. A dozen feet's sprint over jagged rocks depleted that burst of disgusted terror and she jerked to a standstill. She limped back on legs afire with pins and needles, climbed into the truck and stared at his covered head in horrified fascination. She prodded him, her hand recoiling in fear. He still didn't move.

Her doctor side said, Stop his haemorrhage. Survival said, Strip him of weapons and arm yourself. Survival won.

Kneeling by his still body, she searched him for weapons, gaining courage when he didn't move at all. To manoeuvre him on his back, she had to grab and pull and squeeze his body. Then she had to dip her hands under his camouflage jacket to the layers of clothes beneath, undo buttons and zippers and skim cool, velvet-rock muscles to reach the gun where it was shoved deep over his groin.

By the time she'd dragged it away, she was a mass of

agitation. She frowned down at him in confusion. The electricity arcing through her no longer felt like revulsion. It felt like…awareness?

That was it. She *was* concussed. Or getting delusional with hypothermia!

Shaking aside her incredulity, she stared at the gun. She'd fired this very weapon—she snapped a look at her watch—just three hours ago, with the full intention of killing another human being. In self defence, sure, yet…

A shudder shook her from head to toe. *Wallow in recriminations later! If you survive. He could still revive, so you'd better tie him up…*

She paused. The expanding dark red stain now covered his left side. There was no need—no time—to restrain him.

Switching to autopilot resuscitative mode, she aligned his neck. To perform a jaw thrust, to overcome any upper respiratory tract obstruction, she shoved his scarf aside. It fell back—and she did too. On her heels, gaping.

He was…*beautiful.*

The intimidating beauty of a supernatural being from an oriental fable—all polished teak skin, sharp cheekbones and dominant features. And those two amazing silver temple streaks, with their shocking echoes in his raven beard…

Another shudder snapped her out of her stupor. What was she *thinking*? This man was a murderer. He'd most probably be the cause of her own death. He might also die and it would be she who'd killed him. Yet she was wasting vital time taking inventory of his manly assets?

'Escapism! Traumatic delusions…' she muttered to herself as she got back to work and managed to slip his arm from his jacket. But soon she was swearing in impotent rage as the remainder of his layered sleeves resisted her efforts. She was sobbing with frustration when she at last exposed his messy shoulder wound.

Nausea bubbled up again at the sight of her handiwork.

She forced it down and struggled to shred his undershirt for a compression pad and bandage. The other scarf beside him, soaked in dried blood, told its own story. He'd tried to stop his bleeding. But it must have slipped when he'd lost consciousness. Now the arterial bleed was spurting blood with his every powerful heartbeat.

Long, heart-bursting moments later, she had him securely padded and bandaged. She wiped flailing hands on their already bloodied clothes, then forced herself to go through the ABCDE—airway, breathing, circulation and disability. Exposing him to look for other injuries was out of the question, of course.

Apart from his unconsciousness, his vital signs were within acceptable range. Her mind raced. His sympathetic nervous system must be compensating for the heavy blood loss, narrowing his blood vessels to maintain an adequate blood pressure. He was already tachycardic and had tachypnoea—his fast pulse and breathing compensating for the decreased blood volume and pressure. But he *would* deteriorate—and soon.

He had to have immediate blood volume replacement. But *how*, when medical supplies were in the back of the truck, in locked trunks whose combinations still lay with poor, dead Molvich?

Stymied, her eyes returned to his incredible face. She had the ridiculous conviction that if he only woke up, he'd know what to do.

As if in answer to her mental prodding, his heavy lashes fluttered open and his eyes slammed into her.

Gold. Of course. He *had* to have gold eyes.

The inconsequential thought filled her mind as his surprisingly steady gaze mesmerised her. Then he groaned something—in some regional dialect? She thought he'd said, '*Dio mio.*' But that was Italian for 'My God', wasn't it? She must have misheard…

He suddenly moved, and she jumped back and out of the truck, raising the gun, opening her mouth to shout, Don't move.

Then he said one word that shocked her mute.

'*Sherazad?*'

*   *   *

Lorenzo barely caught the woman's stupefied expression before he had to close his eyes again. Looking at her upside down had brought on a suffocating wave of nausea. Oblivion beckoned. He felt so wretched, it almost seemed a good idea to let it claim him again.

Almost.

He couldn't afford the luxury. He had to get this woman to safety, had to stop his deterioration before... He opened his eyes again and calculated the sun's slant by the shadows thrown on the surrounding mountain. It was hours after the ambush. He consulted his body. It hadn't deteriorated as much as it should have with the still heavily bleeding wound... But wait—he wasn't bleeding any more.

He put his right hand to the focus of agony and his surprise doubled. His wound was bandaged. He'd been too disoriented after she'd slammed the door on his head to do more than apply direct pressure to the wound. It hadn't been easy doing even that while driving them away at manic speed—so how...?

Of course. She must have done it. Sherazad. That was the name her companion had screamed to her just before that bloody assassin had shot him down.

He'd been too late for that man. But he'd been determined not to be too late for her. He'd taken the murderer down, tried to get into the truck. And she'd nearly cracked his head open. Tried to rip him to shreds and shot him for his efforts. She'd tried her best to kill him.

Then, judging by the snug bandage, tried her best to save him.

If she thought he was one of the monsters who'd attacked her convoy, why would she bother to save his life now she had him at her mercy?

Weird.

Interesting.

He turned his eyes and met hers. Those incredible, nearly

black eyes that contrasted so much with her rich, creamy complexion and her certainly natural butterscotch hair.

She was now holding the gun in both hands, moving further back as he dragged himself up. He caught a glimpse of himself in the front mirror and grimaced. He looked like a demon out of her land's darkest mythology. It was a miracle she hadn't blasted him away the moment he'd regained consciousness.

'*Ena esh onteem, Sherazad...*' He forced the words through frozen, parched lips, each syllable an agony. Not to mention a total waste. She was clearly unimpressed by his assertions that he was a friend. But wait—no—it was clear she didn't understand.

Strange. His Badovnan was good—so maybe she wasn't Badovnan after all. So what was she, with a name and colouring like that? One of those escaping the new military dictatorship of Azernia, trying to reach a refugee camp or a western European country through the separatist state of Badovna? Had those been Azernian guerrilla forces attacking her convoy? To make an example of deserters? Or Badovnan rebels reinforcing their territory?

No problem. He spoke Azernian too. '*Sho ki siddig, Sherazad. Sho kion mela ossadkom.*'

But again his declarations that he'd been trying to help fell on uncomprehending ears. So what *did* she understand? Was she a deaf-mute, maybe? Had she only read his lips when he'd called her name? He tried every language spoken in the region anyway—Hungarian, Rumanian, Bulgarian, Russian. Her deepening frown indicated that, while she didn't understand, she certainly heard him fine.

English! He'd forgotten English. Most people knew at least a few words, maybe enough for them to communicate.

'After this I'll try sign language,' he said, mainly to himself. 'If you don't understand even that, then I'm stuck. Here goes nothing. Again. Sherazad...' He articulated his words with care, hoping the clarity would make her understand them. 'I am a friend. I was only trying to help.'

Bingo. Her doe eyes widened in what he was certain was comprehension. Then narrowed in sheer disgust and disbelief.

'Think about it.' He leaned back against the driver's seat door, fighting another wave of giddiness. 'If I were one of those butchers, why didn't I just break your neck? You'll remember I only hit you *after* you shot me, to stop you ripping my jugular out…' Her hair suddenly billowed in the wind, revealing the ugly discoloration on the left side of her jaw. He grimaced. 'Ouch!'

Her expression wavered, but not the gun. If anything, both her small hands tightened on it as she took better aim when he struggled to a more upright position. Suddenly, the whole situation struck him as ridiculous.

He'd escaped hundreds of armed-to-the-teeth mercenaries and a dozen deadly situations. He'd crossed the godawful Balkan terrain on foot. He'd been almost home free without so much as a scratch. Now, here he was, concussed, with a bullet in him and about to go into hypovolaemic shock. Even if he didn't, his wound was tightening with the build-up of exudate and the start of infection, and gangrene was inevitable.

All thanks to the woman he'd thought he was saving.

And there she stood, his damsel in distress, covered in his blood, in control, black eyes austere, her glorious mane alive and angry in the wind, with a gun held in a direct line with a point between his eyes.

It was so tragically absurd it was funny.

And he laughed.

Sherazad couldn't believe it.

She was holding him at gunpoint, and he was *laughing*? Why? Was she hiding behind an empty gun? Or did he realise that now she wasn't crazed with fear and fury, she couldn't pull the trigger in cold blood?

Why the *hell* was he laughing?

She was about to scream it out loud when he sobered a

bit. 'I doubt you patched me up only to shoot me again.' His elusively accented baritone again vibrated in her chest, making her bristle. 'So I have two suggestions—get in before you turn into a Popsicle, and let's put our heads together to plan our way out of this predicament.'

When she didn't move, he sighed in resignation, the smile finally leaving his voice. 'Listen, you have the gun, it's loaded, I'm in no shape to try anything funny, even if I wanted to—which I don't. I'm barely keeping my eyes open.'

Sherazad conceded that. He looked awful. And a pang of concern kicked in her gut. She'd treated him only out of a sense of duty—she hadn't felt the least sympathy for him. But now—as his clear-honey eyes turned turbid, and the glow of his bronze complexion faded—*she* felt awful. She felt no better than the monsters who'd killed her companions.

And if it turned out she'd shot the wrong person...

It didn't bear thinking about.

But she couldn't start feeling guilty now, not when he could be playing her for a sucker. Which he probably was!

She weighed the situation, then finally got in, pressing against her door, keeping the eight-foot width of the truck between them, keeping him covered.

'Very prudent.' Again his smile caused an itching sensation behind her breastbone. Her lips thinned at her ridiculous response. She saw his amazing eyes following their movements, felt them there as tangible as a caress. Heat prickled down her spine. What *was* it about this man? What was it with *her*?

'Not talking to me, are you?' He started to shake his head, stopped and groaned—a guttural, thoroughly male sound that resonated in her bones. She seethed, angry with him, enraged at herself. '*Dio mio, signorina*—you've probably given me permanent brain damage.'

So he *had* been speaking Italian! But what was an Italian doing here? Or was he only trying to confuse her? Even if he *was* Italian, Italy was just across the Adriatic from the Balkans. He could be a mercenary or something. He certainly looked the part. Dark and massive and intimidating.

He settled his head back in slow motion, his face shuttered with pain. 'I'm not blaming you, though. You thought you were defending yourself...' He stopped, and the uncanny eyes staring at her dimmed a bit more.

She had no time to analyse her panic as she reached out and checked his carotid pulse. His eyes widened at her action, but she was too absorbed in her assessment to care.

His tachycardia had increased. There was the occasional dropped heartbeat too. He was slipping into shock. She had to install definitive emergency measures *now*.

He said something, but she didn't hear what as she scrambled outside and sprinted around the truck. She snatched open the doors of the twelve-foot van body and rummaged through the stacked trunks, her ears filling with laboured breathing and clanging metal. She dragged the trunk containing IV administration sets and fluids outside, and tried to smash its lock with a rock. All she managed was to batter the metal trunk into an ugly mess.

'What are you doing?' His voice carried to her from the truck, even more subdued. She renewed her efforts, getting frantic.

Suddenly his huge shadow fell over her and she jolted up with a piercing scream.

'*Per Dio*, will you stop being afraid of me? And quit waving that gun in my face? If you kill me, I'd rather you didn't do it accidentally, if you don't mind!'

Was he *joking*? He was!

Well, she failed to see the funny part here. If he was still strong enough to leave the vehicle, he was probably strong enough to overpower her. She summed him up, getting her first good look at his upright physique. Even slumped, his shoulders blocked out her view. He was at least a foot taller than her five feet four, and no doubt twice as heavy. In his normal condition he'd easily be ten times as strong as her.

Now he might still be twice as strong. And many men thought it only natural to settle disputes with weaker individuals—especially women—through violence.

She waved him back with the gun and he sighed. 'I only staggered here to see if I could help. You *know* you have nothing to fear from me. Even if you don't believe me, I have one useless arm and you'd probably blow me away if you sneeze. So, what's so desperately important inside that trunk? More weapons? Was that why you were attacked? Were you trafficking weapons? But why would *you* want more weapons now? All you need is one more bullet to finish me.'

She gaped at him. His cultured voice, his eloquent English, which clearly wasn't his mother tongue, struck her again. They indicated a high level of intelligence and education—not to be expected of a sleazy mercenary. She was even more stunned by his interpretation of her convoy's mission. Was *that* why they were attacked? For free and sorely needed arms? Though, if word of their mission had leaked out, medical supplies were just as valuable.

'Not that the weapons theory holds water.' He too seemed to be looking for a better explanation, summing her up in turn. 'You don't fit the profile of an arms dealer, especially since you can't even fire a weapon properly, *grazie Dio*!' His right hand rubbed his jaw in a thoughtful motion—then he removed it with startled expression. It was as if he didn't expect to find hair there!

Now, what did that mean? What did it tell her? She replayed his every word, gesture and expression in her mind. Her observations were all she had to help her decide what he really was.

At her continued silence he sighed again. 'Oh, whatever. What the hell—play the sphinx if you insist. Let me see what I can do to get this thing open.'

He knelt by the trunk and assessed the lock and the inefficiency of her efforts to break it, then looked up. 'Only a combination or a bullet will get this open. You clearly only have the second.'

She shook her head in horror. She wasn't firing this monstrous gun again. She'd probably blow off her leg!

'*Bene.*' He nodded as if he'd read her thoughts and agreed to her fears. 'I wouldn't advise using the gun if your experience with guns started and ended with blasting a hole in me. The recoil alone would make you miss—at best. I have that to thank for being alive. You aimed at the heart and, even at a foot away, got the shoulder...' He paused, caught a breath that was becoming shallower and quicker. Then he tried again. 'I can do it.'

She jumped back again, shaking her head, all her doubts crashing back. Do her a favour and take the gun, her only protection? How convenient! And how stupid did he think she was?

He gave a have-it-your-way shrug and started to struggle to his feet. But he staggered and fell forward, slumping on the trunk.

Her heart pounded as she watched him squeeze his eyes and strive for enough strength and co-ordination to get up.

If they didn't get that trunk open, he wouldn't last long. He'd lost too much blood and his body's compensatory mechanisms were almost exhausted. His blood pressure must be falling, and soon all his vital systems would begin to fail. Then he'd enter a vicious circle, leading to irreversible shock and death.

She had three choices. Waste the gun's ammunition trying to blast the lock, probably fail, maybe add more injuries to their quandary, and watch him die. Hold onto the weapon and watch him die. *Or*—trust her instincts...

She placed a hand on his shoulder as he finally straightened. He looked up in surprise, which turned to stupefaction when she extended the gun to him. Their eyes met, locked. Too many things, too complex for words, buzzed between them in that gaze.

Then, with a gentle nod, he reached out and took the gun. 'Stand back.'

She obeyed and watched him uncoil to his full daunting height, swaying a few feet back himself. Once she was far enough away, he took a shuddering breath. She could almost feel the effort he was expending to steady his hand. Then he fired. The lock exploded apart. The crack of thunder ricocheted off the mountains, enclosing them in echoes.

When they at last died away, he raised unreadable eyes to hers and panic swamped her. What had she done? She'd given him her gun! He could have helped her because he *did* believe the trunk was full of weapons. What if he turned on her? What if—?

Then he smiled and her fears vanished as if they had never been. She'd been right to trust him. Not only that, but suddenly she felt safe and protected. It was stupid, but it was how his smile made her feel.

He beckoned and extended the gun back to her, butt first. She didn't take it but rushed to drag out more trunks. She needed supplies and instruments out of each. Without a word, he shot their locks off, checked the gun's remaining load, then handed it back to her.

'You have eight rounds left—save them for the deserving.' He tried to deliver the jab with a smile, but failed. His face was now pinched with pain and depletion, his teeth clattering with cold. He swayed back to the truck and dragged himself inside, and she swooped to gather all she needed.

She rushed back to the truck to find him slumped at the door, shivering all over, his eyes closed. The moment he felt her slide in beside him, he mumbled without opening his eyes, 'Can you drive?'

What? What did it matter to him if she could drive? Drive *where*, for heaven's sake? They were in the middle of nowhere.

If that wasn't enough, he needed a trauma surgeon, not an A and E doctor like her. She had studied Dr Banducci's comprehensive notes targeting GAO volunteer doctors, stressing field injuries. But she hadn't expected to put them to practice so soon, or in these conditions. What if she didn't remember how to do anything? What if she really no longer had it in her to handle emergencies?

She tried to squash her insecurities as she covered him with her blanket, mentally ticking off the measures needed to stabilise him. But the malignant thoughts percolated, until she almost screamed at herself, *Stop it. You can't call your consultant now. You can't quit—again!*

His groan penetrated her agitation. 'Don't tell me you suddenly don't understand me again. In case you're giving me the silent treatment because you *still* don't trust me, let me introduce myself. I'm Dr Lorenzo Alessandro Banducci, head of Global Aid Organisation's aid missions in the Balkans…'

CHAPTER TWO

HER abductor was still talking.

But Sherazad had stopped listening.

She could hear nothing above the pounding in her head. See nothing beyond the blackness closing in on her.

Was she going to faint?

Did he actually say *he* was Dr Banducci? The internationally renowned Italian surgeon who'd been heading volunteer medical relief operations in war zones all over the world for the past six years? Who'd disappeared two months ago without a trace? Whose disappearance was still causing worldwide outrage?

No. *No*—he couldn't be.

He must be one of the doctor's kidnappers. That would explain how he knew of Dr Banducci. And now he was using his knowledge to impersonate him, to confuse her, to—to…

Her feverish thoughts skidded to a halt as she stared in horror at the regal profile inches from her face.

Despite his dishevelment, this wasn't the face of a monster. And it had nothing to do with his incredible good looks. Thorough breeding stamped his every feature, mercy and compassion showed in his every expression.

She'd seen one photo of Dr Banducci in a newspaper, in surgical scrubs and cap. That one-of-a-kind hair could have been covered. The astonishing colour of his eyes wouldn't have shown in the muddy print. He'd also been clean-shaven, but two months on the run could account for the beard. The beard he wasn't used to having…

He was who he said he was.

And she'd shot him.

He could die.

No! Not if she had anything to do about it.

'...your unmarked trucks, so I didn't know who I'd be helping. But I had to help anyway.'

Her attention snapped back in time to hear his last sentence. If not to make sense of it. She croaked, 'Pardon?'

He opened his eyes, turned his head and stared at her for a full minute. Then his face crumpled. On feeble, agonised...*laughter*.

'*Pardon?*' he gasped. '*Dio mio. Una Inglese.* Only an Englishwoman would say "Pardon" after I've poured out every detail of my last nightmarish two months! The two months crowned by her nearly killing me!'

Did he have to remind her? Her guilt and dread had become unbearable and she hated the emotions. She'd lived with them for too long. But she no longer bore them in silence. Now they only made her angry. 'Oh, shut up! Stop blabbing and conserve your energy.'

Her vehemence cut short his laughter, though his eyes kept smiling. Those eyes that seemed to be shining a light from within him... She averted hers to place the IV equipment on the dashboard and rip off packaging.

'Who are you, *mi piccola* Miss Nightingale?'

'As if knowing who I am would make the slightest difference.' Considering the subject closed, she again struggled to roll up his sleeves. He tugged at her, stopping her, silently demanding an answer.

'For heaven's sake, let me get some fluids in you...' The blurted out words died on her lips. His were mere inches away, and his breath, surprisingly fresh yet so...potent, tickled her lips, filling her lungs with his masculine aroma.

Would he taste as good?

Snapping exasperated eyes up, to escape the insane urge to close the gap and find out, she found herself snared instead by the gentle probing of his compelling gaze. From the frying-pan into the fire.

'OK,' she said between her teeth. 'If it's more important

to you than not going into shock! I was part of the medical team that was supposed to take the first GAO field operation into the region since your—since Dr Banducci's—disappearance. We were supposed to reach a military base, take a helicopter to liaise at GAO's headquarters, then head for the Sredna refugee camp. So, if you're *truly* Dr Banducci, then you're my new boss!'

Lorenzo Banducci's eyes, if it was really him, widened as he relaxed his persuasive hold on her and slumped into his original pose. He wheezed a weak chuckle. 'I know I didn't want new posts in my Badovnan operation, but that was no reason to shoot me on sight.'

'You didn't want…?' What was he talking about? There was always a desperate need for qualified volunteer doctors in aid work. In his operation especially, which no one seemed keen to volunteer for on account of its higher danger factor.

Her confusion didn't last long, for he explained, his voice a mere whisper now. 'Before I was abducted, I had an efficient core team, which I wanted to keep on the move without the burden of having to train rookies. But I did agree in the end…'

A massive shudder engulfed him, and she jumped to tuck the blanket around him, wrapping his scarf and hers around his head, a major source of heat loss. She spared an awed blink at his arms as she snapped tourniquets on both, inserted cannulae, attached Ringer's lactate solution tubes to them, released the tourniquets and set the drip to macro mode for the quickest possible fluid replacement.

He seemed oblivious of her actions, his eyes fogging as he talked—to himself, it seemed. 'So GAO resumed operations, even when they gave up on my return! I hoped they would. Suspending activities played right into my abductors' hands. But going with an unmarked convoy as a decoy was no use to anyone. Neither was your armed escort. Those trunks are full of prepackaged medical kits, aren't they? A veritable moving hospital, no doubt with a complete surgical theatre! Reason enough for *any* of the warring factions to attack you…'

Another violent shudder interrupted him, before he continued, his voice slurring. 'I learned of the attack when a man I helped told me not to take that road at that time. I tried to intercept your convoy, but I was too late.' He stopped, frowned. 'If they attacked you, knowing you were a medical convoy, they might have spared some of your colleagues, to put them to work, patching up *their* wounded. They probably would have spared you—if not for your medical prowess…' His pained eyes roamed over her and nausea kicked in her gut.

What would have happened to her had he not saved her?

A whimper escaped her, making him wince and reach a trembling hand to her bruised jaw. He couldn't hold it up and it dropped heavily to his side.

'I'm glad I got to you first,' he gasped. 'Even if you might have killed me for my efforts…'

Her breath hitched with fright. 'No! You're going to be fine. I'll take care of you.'

'Haven't you taken care of me already?'

She couldn't believe it. He was at irreversible shock's door and his sense of humour hadn't even waned. At least this boded well for the absence of intracranial injuries from that three-hundred-pound door to the head!

He sighed. 'You've a light touch. I didn't feel those needles. Mind you, I'm probably too numb with hypothermia and shock. So—are you a medic or a nurse?'

'As in women can't possibly be doctors?' It was stupid to bristle this way, in these circumstances, but she'd *had* it with all forms of condescension, manipulation and oppression. She'd sworn she'd never put up with any for one more second of her life.

'I assure you, I attend Male Chauvinist Pigs Anonymous regularly.' He sounded so serious that for a second she took his words seriously. Then they sank in. And she did the last thing she'd thought possible in this harrowing situation.

She burst out laughing.

Her laughter had a strange effect on him. He sobered completely.

'Christo, piccola, ma tu il più carina…' The Italian words came out scalding, the rolling r's and stressed l's—his foreign origin's only indications—sending a hot, rough caress sweeping through her.

He was saying she was beautiful. Even if she hadn't understood the words, his deeply male gaze said it all. After Jack's rabid eyes on her, she hated to be seen as female. Her laughter died abruptly.

'Your fluid deficit's been taken care of, so it's time to take care of your wound.' She ignored his almost tactile gaze, and tried to project crisp professionalism. Inside she was quailing. It had been over a year since she'd handled as much as a paper-cut. 'And if you're really Dr Lorenzo Banducci, you'll tell me what I'm supposed to do next.'

'Are you verifying my identity, or just grabbing a quick refresher course in wound management?' His teasing tones were much steadier. It seemed he was reviving already.

She glared at him and he rolled his eyes in merry surrender. Her lips twitched. There was no staying mad at the man!

'Bene.' He inclined his awesome head, sitting up a bit. 'Gunshot wounds: principles of surgical management. All wounds must be explored. All wounds must be debrided. All dead tissue must be excised. Ah, by the way, what instruments do you have to handle the mess? Ideally, I'd use tissue forceps, delicate scissors, non-crushing vascular clamps, scalpel handle and blade, skin retractor, various sutures—and a standard regional anaesthesia tray. When all's prepared, you release pressure, and pray the bleeding has stopped. But, given my luck, the bullet probably ripped the head honcho itself, the axillary artery, so you'd better be prepared for some fancy fountain works and be quick with clamping and suture ligation.'

'All right. Fine! So you are who you say you are!' He

had to go for overkill, didn't he? She huffed as she snapped on gloves, and he grinned, that arrhythmia-inducing grin of his. She couldn't let him get away with it. '*Or* you may be one of Dr Banducci's theatre staff, a cleaning man or something, who's picked up all that information in years of hero-worshipping service to the great surgeon.'

'*Grazie, grazie*. No need to kneel to the great surgeon, really!'

She conceded another fact: there was no getting the better of him when it came to comebacks either.

She spread her packaged, pre-sterilised tools on sterile gauze on the wide dashboard, placed the syringes, drug bottles and ampoules next to them, then drew in a breath. To her mortification, it was almost a sob.

Lorenzo's gentle hand came up under her chin, and persuaded her eyes up to his. 'You don't have to do this.' His voice was serious now, kind.

She raised an incredulous eyebrow. 'Oh, really? You may not have picked me for your team, but I assure you your strict selection standards were maintained. I graduated among the top five in my year and was an A and E registrar in my last post. So spare me the movie heroics that you can bear it like a man.'

'I only meant I can do it myself,' he said, animation surging back into his face by the second. 'With the help of the excellent nursing staff of yourself and Head Nurse Morphine.' He finished with a wink.

'Don't you ever stop joking? Or is that the concussion talking? You know you can't do that, not with one hand, even if it is your magical operating hand, Mr Godly Surgeon.'

'Actually, it isn't. I'm left-handed, Dr Sherazad Touchy.'

That silenced her. She'd shot him in the arm attached to his precise surgeon's hand!

'No need to worry, Sherazad. I can do it.' His tone held such compassion that she wanted to scream. Why must he be kind? How could he be? Even if his life was no longer in immediate danger, his arm was. She might have cost him his arm. His most valuable possession.

Guilt made her belligerent. 'No, you can't. And I'm *not* giving you morphine. Surely a surgeon of your calibre knows centrally depressant drugs are contra-indicated in a prime head-injury suspect like yourself!'

'You mean you're going to dissect me alive *and* aware? I've seen all sorts of war atrocities, but vivisection is just too barbarous.'

She stamped her foot. 'Oh, for God's sake. Stop joking! How *can* you joke?'

Ignore him, she told herself. *Get your medications ready.* She did until his soft question made her drop the Lidocaine ampoule.

'How many times have you treated a wound that size and extracted a bullet, Sherazad?'

'How do you know my name?' Suddenly it seemed all-important to know. He told her. She winced as the memory of those macabre moments hit her between the eyes.

He again raised her chin with a soft finger, his voice soothing, hypnotic. 'We joke, Sherazad, to keep on being of any use to anyone. Starting with ourselves.'

Suddenly it was too much. Not only what had happened in the past hours, but in the past years. She hadn't cried through any of it. Not once. The more insanity she'd faced, the drier her eyes had become. Now his empathy, his quiet understanding, his implied sharing of suffering had tears forcing their way out of burning eyes and raining down frozen cheeks.

She tried to escape the fingers under her chin, but they came up to cup her cheek, dipping into her tears, smoothing them away. 'I don't need my surgeon's eyes blurred. Or are all those tears to irrigate my wound? Don't you have saline, *piccola*?'

There was no staying down around him either.

She shook her head, tears mingling with smiles. 'Will you stop calling me *piccola*? I'm not small—*you're* huge!'

'So you know Italian!'

'The odd word. And regardless of my size or what you think is my comparative medical expertise, I can handle this.'

'Uh…about anaesthesia…?'

'I thought we agreed!'

'*You* agreed!'

'Don't worry, I'm not totally stupid. See this?' She wiggled the syringe she'd just loaded with Lidocaine. 'I'm using infiltration anaesthesia!'

'For a wound that deep, *piccola*, you'll need enough Lidocaine to kill me before it will block out pain.'

She paused in horror. He was right. Recovering quickly, she said, 'I wasn't about to exceed the maximum permissible dose.'

He still shook his head. 'The bullet is lodged pretty deep. For effective block, you'd still have to inject so deep your permissible dose would have a toxic effect.'

'And you're the one suggesting morphine!'

He leaned back and gave her an easy smile. 'I suggested enough to dull the pain, not to have me tripping. In fact, pain would keep me informed of my arm's functions. I also want to be somewhere outside the twilight zone to guide you through any surprises. But you're right. Right now, even a minimum dose might have me irreversibly comatose.'

'Any other suggestions, then, other than having you bite down on the headrest?' She strove to sound light, even though her blood was freezing just thinking of his possible deterioration. She could handle it, she'd said? *Ha.*

'You could recount one of your thousand and one tales, Sherazad. It always numbed Sherayar effectively, didn't it?'

'I was waiting for you to make some crack about my name. How predictable!'

He wasn't in the least abashed. 'Your name *is* irresistible. And fitting. But you, my modern-day Sherazad, if you can't control a beast with your wiles, you blast him apart.'

'Will you stop reminding me?'

'Don't feel *too* bad. I've forgiven you.'

He was toying with her, the fiend. *The gravely injured fiend.*

Her face fell at the reminder. As if she could forget. Though he *did* make her forget, not only their clear and present danger but that she'd only known him an hour. That she didn't even want to *look* at men any more.

'We return to the question of anaesthesia. So, you tell me. A lengthy and agonising shoulder procedure. What anaesthetic technique would be best?'

She couldn't believe the man. They were in the worst situation of her life, probably the worst of his, and he was examining her knowledge like her consultant on a ward round!

'Do I get points in your assessment if I answer correctly?'

'It can be arranged.' He nodded, then winked. 'Though I'd prefer to kiss you for your cleverness.'

'I'll take the points.'

'Spoilsport.' He pouted in mock reproach. 'So…?'

She groped desperately for the optimum anaesthetic procedure. But every bit of medical knowledge had evaporated.

Then it hit her. She couldn't believe she'd not thought of it from the start. If he'd been unconscious, if he'd been any other patient, she would have probably committed all sorts of fatal blunders! Mortified by her serious lapse, she muttered the answer through her teeth. 'Brachial plexus block.'

'Excellente, piccola!' Her gaze narrowed on him, but there wasn't the slightest sarcasm in his. He even looked surprised that she knew. 'And do you know how it's done?'

'We inject Lidocaine or a longer-acting anaesthetic in the lower neck, where the brachial plexus that supplies nerves to the shoulder and arm lies in a superficial sheath in the interscalene groove, between the anterior and middle scalene muscles, just above the clavicle, the collar-bone.'

'Perfetto.' His eyes gleamed with uncanny perception. 'But you've never done one?'

'No!'

'Don't be so defensive. As an A and E doctor, you naturally leave definitive procedures to surgeons and anaesthetists. Now you're in the field you'll get used to managing a casualty from A to Z. As for now, we're working together. First, let me check...'

For the next two minutes he performed every known neurological exam on his arm, then at last said, 'OK, you have one neurologically sound arm to work with. Now to keep it that way.'

In a minute he was lying on his back, his head facing away from the side to be blocked, his neck slightly stretched.

As she prepared the skin with iodine, he cleared his throat. 'Um, I'd appreciate a needle insertion site anaesthesia—with a 25-gauge needle, please.'

'I'm not a total moron!' She injected the anaesthetic, fighting the temptation to jab him with it, only to find him gazing sideways at her with that velvet smile of his. Her tension dissolved into an answering and, no doubt, idiotic grin. 'I even remembered that once the sheath is located, a needle can slip out if I fumble for a catheter. So, here's the catheter, ready for insertion *before* beginning the procedure.'

His grin widened. 'Textbook precision. I'm more impressed by the second.'

This man is dangerous. The thought burst in her mind, becoming a certainty in a heartbeat. *This man is* lethal. *She'd better watch him.*

Watch herself.

Returning to her crucial task with a severe mental smack, she identified the brachial plexus, then followed his detailed directions for needle placement into its sheath.

'Parasthesia's nice and constant.' That meant the needle elicited burning or a pins-and-needles sensation in his arm, indicating she was in the right place. 'Good job, Sherazad. Now inject. I'll let you know if parasthesia stops.'

She knew if this happened, her injection would be going astray. She injected very slowly, holding her breath for him to deliver bad news. He didn't. Instead, he delivered vital guidance. In teasing form, granted, but it still filled her with assurance, kept her on the right track.

'Aspirate as you inject, *piccola*. Let's not have an accidental intravascular or intrathecal injection in this place. I'm not done with this mortal coil yet!'

He meant it would be fatal if the injection entered the circulation through an artery or the cerebrospinal fluid through the sheath around the spinal cord. But she already knew that, knew how to make sure it didn't happen, and it boosted her confidence greatly. She finished injecting 45 ml of Lidocaine and teased back. 'And I don't want to get rid of you—yet!'

His answering smile was as debilitating as ever. 'Now simultaneously withdraw the needle and advance the catheter. You *did* intend to leave the catheter in for pain management afterwards, didn't you?'

She secured the catheter with tape and gave him her best withering look.

It only won her another wink as he sat up, purring his appreciation. 'Hmm, nice and numb.' She tried to make him lie down again, but he overrode her. 'We're a team, remember? Now to assess the damage to the shoulder.'

Sherazad marvelled at his calmness. *The* shoulder, he'd said, not *my* shoulder. He didn't seem worried what the examination might reveal.

Jack would have been frantic over a splinter.

She shook away the bitter recollections as Lorenzo removed his bandages and inspected his wound in the setting sun's weakening light. It gushed again and she jumped into clamp and suture ligation, squeezing the bleeders closed with a clamp and keeping them that way with stitches.

He watched her work in silence, then finally spoke, his voice rumbling in amusement. 'I take back anything bad I said about my luck. Not only have I stumbled across a princess from oriental mythology, saved her from the barbarians and she turned out to be a healer who performs the quickest clamp-ligation on record, but my main arteries are intact.' He paused as he finger-explored his wound for its extent and for any lodged foreign objects while she irrigated it thoroughly with saline. 'So are my rotator cuff and shoulder joint.'

Relief flooded through her on a tidal wave. But instead of breathing easily again, she was two breaths away from hyperventilation. It was his praise and the deepening awareness tugging at her... She needed a distraction!

His wound, the one she'd inflicted on him, provided plenty of that.

'But your deltoid muscle is blasted.'

He shrugged. 'The famed flesh wound.'

'Oh, stop it! How can you be so nonchalant? You know how easily I can get this wrong. Either cut out too much good muscle and cause you a disability, or leave in too much bad and cause you hideous complications—anything from renal failure to gas gangrene!'

'You sure know your trauma medicine, Sherazad.' He whistled, not at all fazed by her projections. And she nearly smacked herself for real.

What was she *doing*, regaling her patient with horrific visions of worst-case scenarios?

But he wasn't any 'patient'. He knew far more than she did about it all. And he seemed unconcerned. So what did he know that she didn't? Or was he simply so hardened by his years in war zones that no injury disturbed him any longer? Not even his own?

'These have to go.' His calm words snapped her eyes to the most traumatised muscles, confirming her assessment. 'Start snipping.'

'Will you at least look away while I do that?' She couldn't bear imagining what it must be like for him to watch his flesh being cut off and thrown away.

His hand again cupped her cheek, his capable surgeon's

fingers stroking her. Then suddenly he dipped his head and replaced his fingers with his lips, and her skin caught fire.

'Don't worry about me, *piccola*.' His voice reverberated against her flesh, spearing through her like a bolt of lightning. She shuddered and he withdrew to look at her—into her.

She stared at him, aching for his reassurance, his forgiveness and, above all, his closeness. The ultimate safety of his flesh on hers.

He must have understood, for he came back to her, giving her all she needed.

Lorenzo had to be close to this magnificent creature, needed to bask in her compassion, to soothe her. He had the ridiculous conviction that having her flesh on his was even more crucial to his survival than treating his wound.

He touched his lips to that flushed, petal-soft mouth, as he'd been aching to ever since she'd bitten him during the struggle. He caught that lower, tender lip between his and bit down gently. It trembled, then her mouth opened to him, yielding a taste and moist warmth that swamped him. Her deep, satin voice quivered in a moan of—what? Urgency? Apprehension? Surrender? He absorbed it inside him with a groan of reassurance, coaxing her. He plunged into the tender recesses of her mouth, enraptured, as time slowed and the world fell away...

The IV line snagged on his right arm. He couldn't feel his left one.

What was he doing?

He couldn't even hold her. He couldn't possibly be this aroused. He'd only known her an hour. They were stranded. In mortal danger. And in the middle of a critical surgical procedure.

He couldn't even put the foregoing in order of importance.

He *must* be suffering a more severe concussion than he'd thought.

As if by agreement, they drew apart at the same instant. For seconds, the stunned hunger in her eyes nearly made him drag her back to him, and to hell with everything. But a second later, her gaze went blank, making him doubt what he'd seen there. Then with a frown of supreme concentration, she went to work, dissecting a careful path to the bullet.

Satisfied with her performance, his gaze went to her face.

Had he said she was beautiful? She wasn't. Neither was she even conventionally pretty. She was beyond such common descriptions.

That translucent skin, that hundred-shades hair, those sculpted bones and features. But it was her onyx eyes that made her unique. Fathomless eyes, windows to depths he wanted to plunder, to plunge into and lose himself…

His libido and his incredulity soared as one.

He might be unable to function as a surgeon again. They might not survive this mess for that to even be an issue. And all he could think of was this woman, hot and wet and naked and clasped around him as he gave her pleasure and drew his from hers! He laughed. She tensed, but kept on working.

Once she'd finished, she raised disapproving eyes. 'Although I'm not impressed with your weird sense of humour, I am with your anatomy textbook muscles. This way I'm sure I didn't damage their insertions or nerve-blood supply as I extracted this.' She held the bullet up for his inspection.

'Let's see if you've left me enough muscles for *those* to be of any use.'

A strange sound issued from her, and his eyes flew to her face. The distress he saw there…! She really abhorred harming another human being. No matter who he was. The pain *had* been there, even when she'd thought him a murderer. And he'd been teasing her about it non-stop!

Feeling like the most insensitive lout on earth, he tried to make amends. 'Don't mind me, Sherazad. I'm just a thoughtless wretch. Actually, I think you've been too conservative. I think more snipping is in order.'

'No!' She curbed her horror with a visible effort, then added in a more controlled voice, 'Relying on the Four Cs guideline—colour, contraction, consistency and circulation—I think these muscles are good and they can stay.'

He met her eyes. They pleaded with him to support her verdict. He looked at his blasted shoulder again, and weighed his options. Removing more would cause too much scar tissue and contracture, and would cripple him. Right now, his remaining muscles would hypertrophy, enlarge to reform the lost bulk and restore any diminished function. They didn't look unacceptable, just a…bit equivocal. He decided to leave them in and take his chances.

She took his silence for agreement and with a tremulous exhalation cut the ragged skin edges, opened the wound deeply to allow for thorough drainage, then finally paused to look at him. He sensed she was seeking his approval.

He gave it to her in actions, applying sterile gauze followed by a bulky non-occlusive dressing, ending the procedure. 'You must be itching to suture me up but you'll have to leave me open for the wound to drain. Primary closure of a wound of that calibre is in four to ten days.'

'I know that!'

He gave her his best mock-innocent smile as he held the bandaging in his teeth and started wrapping his shoulder. 'You do?'

'Will you stop yanking my chain? Oh, let me do that.'

A minute later, he objected. 'Don't mummify me yet! And no splint or sling. I need to put this arm to use as soon as anaesthesia wears off.'

'Is this a macho thing?' Aggravation dripped from her voice as she loosened the bandages and began again. 'Exacerbated and complicated by your Latin genes? Wanting to do everything yourself, wanting to use your arm when you know proper immobilisation is mandatory?'

He couldn't stop teasing her. He was just having too much fun with their verbal volleys. 'Kindly remember who's the surgeon and war-injuries expert here, *innamorata.*

'And though you did do a meticulous job, want to bet I'd have done as good a job unaided?'

'Don't tempt me to leave you to the rest of said job.'

'Why don't you? Or are you afraid you'd lose the bet? You might want to lose. You already enjoyed the stakes I have in mind.'

Even in the truck's dim lighting, that skin gave her away. She must have known, for she didn't try to dispute her crimson confession.

'Just remember that *imagined* sexual attraction is a survival mechanism in seemingly hopeless situations!'

'Oh, sure. And I have a teleportation device to sell you. The fireworks couldn't be more real, *tesoro*. The situation just accelerated admitting them, acting on them.'

'For God's sake! Is this the famous Italian sexuality? I can't believe I'm going to work for you. You're impossible.'

'If you don't have some hard-hitting antibiotics, I doubt you'll have me to work for in a few days.'

'And if we remain here, or if the guerrillas catch up with us, I won't be available to work for anyone either.'

Oppressive silence descended. And, again, too many emotions and things to say commuted wordlessly between them.

It was Sherazad who broke the silent connection, going back to work, injecting him with broad-spectrum antibiotics, anti-inflammatories and a tetanus booster. She hung another bag of Ringer's lactate on his left arm and disconnected the one on his right, leaving the cannula in place. Then she began to reassess his status. He waited until she was taking his radial pulse, then tugged her to him again, pressing her into his much larger body, containing her. She didn't even try to pull away. She just let out a ragged exhalation and burrowed into him.

He hugged her tight and rubbed his cheek where it was hair-free over her mink-soft head, inhaling her freshness and breathing his reassurance into her hair. 'I'm fine. You've saved me—and my arm.'

'Have I?' She sounded desperately worried still, and he couldn't help it. He just had to reassure her.

Tilting her face up, he closed her frantic eyes with a feather-tender kiss on each. 'You have...' Then he trailed those same kisses down her nose to her lips.

Her cold lips hesitated under his coaxing for a second, then melted and allowed his entry, burying him in an avalanche of sensations. Hot, powerful, pure. Reason said it was a huge mistake. But what did reason matter any more? How could they fight—*this*? Why? What if they died tomorrow? They needed this, wherever it took them. Now. Come what may...

A loud crack penetrated their crashing heartbeats and laboured breathing. They snapped apart. He lunged over her and reached for the gun. Snatching off his IV tubing, he snapped off the cabin light and darted looks around the windows. He saw nothing.

He cursed low and fluently in Italian. It was another moonless night and they must have been sitting targets inside the lighted truck.

Sherazad protested his protective position, her protests getting louder when he started getting out of the truck. He hushed her.

'I must take higher ground. I may still have a minute. There's only one way out of here, and they'll be blocking it now. Get under that blanket and keep totally still. Don't come out for any reason. They may be few enough for me to get them all. If I don't, turn the truck around and blast your way out of here.'

CHAPTER THREE

'YOU'RE *not* going out there.' Sherazad clung to Lorenzo with a strength he was no match for at the moment. 'Either we both stay, or I go. I'm the healthy one.'

'And I'm the—'

'The man?' she completed in distraught exasperation.

'The one who can use a gun. But you've cost me the minute's head start. Now I have to make a stand here.' He squeezed her arm, and they froze, listening for an attack. All they heard was the wind lamenting in the narrow ravine around them.

At last, after what felt like an eternity, he closed the door and turned on the light, his mind racing. He shared his thoughts with her as they formed. 'I think we heard a boulder rolling off the mountain. Not attackers, but boulders can be just as fatal. I thought we'd remain here until daylight, but we must move out now. This gale will bring down more boulders. We'll be out in the open, but maybe the Azernian guerrillas, if it was them who attacked you, won't venture that far for one more truck, not that...' He let the rest dwindle into an inaudible undertone.

'What was that?' she asked in alarm.

'Don't worry about it.'

'Now I'm more worried—if that's possible. What *is* it?'

'If you insist, I said Badovnan rebels aren't that safer a bet to run into!'

A strangled laugh escaped her. 'From one frying-pan to another, then.'

'We'll see.' His chuckle was somehow relaxed. After all he'd been through, he felt up to facing anything. He ruffled

36

her hair, started the engine and turned the heater on full blast.

'So you *didn't* run out of fuel!' she exclaimed as he put the vehicle in motion, just now realising it, it seemed. 'Why didn't you turn on the heater before? Did you fancy getting a combination of frostbite and shock?'

'I thought I shouldn't use up the battery or the fuel. That is, when I could think at all. I was a bit preoccupied, if you'll remember—hearing echoes of a door slamming on my head, a bullet in my shoulder, having a gun waved in my face and various needles and scalpels stuck into me. Then there was the mind-numbing bliss…'

'Stop the truck!' Sherazad's abrupt order had him braking in surprise, a surprise that soared when she climbed over him. His heart lurched in a crazy mixture of astonishment and excitement. The next moment he realised she was only replacing him at the wheel, easing him along the bench seat with utmost care. He laughed out loud at his wishful thinking.

She didn't comment on his laughter, just put the truck in motion and said, 'To answer your much earlier question, yes, I can drive—anything from a motorcycle to a bus to an eighteen-wheeler.'

'Collecting such an unlikely driving résumé must be one of your fascinating thousand and one tales, Sherazad.'

Sherazad didn't answer him as she concentrated on manoeuvring the brutal terrain, holding her breath as they neared the entrance of the chasm.

The moment they emerged onto open ground he said, 'Stop and turn off the headlights.' She complied at once, and he explained, 'I need to see the stars to navigate.'

She hadn't even thought how they'd find their way. Star navigation definitely wouldn't have occurred to her. 'Is this how you found your way after you escaped?'

'Yes—until I was far enough from my mountain prison. That was the first three weeks' journey.'

It impressed her beyond words that he could do that. She

pictured herself lost here, alone or with anyone she knew—Jack, for instance. They wouldn't have known the first thing about finding their way, or fending for themselves. Modern people seemed to have forgotten the basics of survival outside the cocoon of technology and modern facilities. But Lorenzo Banducci hadn't lost touch with the old ways, it seemed. He'd survive in any conditions. He already had.

'I did ask for directions occasionally, shortcuts mainly,' he continued, snapping her out of her musings. 'It pays to know the local languages. Go this way.'

Her eyes had adapted to the level of darkness so she drove on, following his pointing finger. 'And the natives were helpful?'

'Sometimes.' She heard the smile in his deep baritone, felt it caressing her again. 'You really didn't hear a word when I chronicled my great escape.'

'I was a bit shocked at the time.'

'You and me both.'

Now they were over that crisis, she could laugh at his pun. Still smiling, she asked, 'So what happened? Who kidnapped you and why? And why didn't they announce responsibility for your disappearance? Everyone thought you were killed.'

'They didn't tell me who they were, and spoke to me in broken English, so I can only speculate. As to why, I think they kidnapped me to stop the aid operations in the region, to plunge it into more chaos. Whoever they were, they must have been too embarrassed to broadcast their failure to hold me. It's why I'm so determined to survive, so I can expose them, let people know that the oppressors who're manipulating their lives and dragging them through war can be beaten, that their only power is in others' silence and surrender, others' lack of knowledge, discipline and initiative.'

She took her eyes off the road to stare at him. In the dim light of bright stars she saw a new Lorenzo Banducci. Impassioned. Intense. The emotions blazing on his face disturbed her in a way nothing ever had. Her throat convulsed and unaccountable tears stung her eyes.

Desperate to lighten the mood, she teased, 'Are you planning on changing your vocation from doctor to political leader? Which side will you champion then?'

He turned on her, and for the first time she knew he was angry. Livid. 'I don't acknowledge politics, ideologies or orientations. All I care about is that it's the same in every ravaged place on earth I've been. A dishonourable war with civilians as the only sufferers, *all* the parties powermongering and guilty, the rest of the world contributing to the catastrophe. All I want is to penetrate the politics to reach out to the forgotten and forsaken. Don't taint me with the leanings you've formed in the safety of ignorance and the luxury of unbreachable civil rights. You, who'll never know what desperation means, what oppression is, coming here all smug and superior, to charitably and *temporarily* tend to the downtrodden…'

He trailed off, fell silent for a moment, then muttered a string of low, furious Italian words to himself. At last he drew in a ragged breath. '*Piccola*, I'm sorry…' He reached for her when she didn't react. 'Sherazad, please…' His right hand trailed from her cheek to her arm, caressing her in entreaty, his voice softening, darkening. 'That was…inexcusable. You've already proved through a brutal test that you're caring and undiscriminating—*too* humane, really. You've transcended terror and violence—the very urgings of survival—and helped your apparent enemy. Forgive me.'

She couldn't bear his apologies or his praise. He'd been right the first time. Her motives for being here were far from noble. She attempted to laugh it off. 'Don't nominate me for sainthood yet. You don't know the first thing about me.'

'I know what you did. It's enough.'

His quiet conviction embarrassed her even more. She had to set him straight. 'Here's a different viewpoint. I woke up and found myself in the middle of nowhere. I thought I was dead if the man who was bleeding all over me died before he showed me the way out. I had the gun and the upper hand, so I patched him up!'

He was silent for a long moment. In the end, curiosity got the better of her and she turned to him. She saw a set of strong, white teeth gleaming in the dark.

'You really have the most atrocious sense of humour! Does everything I say pass through your brain and come out funny?'

In answer to that, he burst out laughing. Peal after peal of cruelly masculine laughter. Just when she felt about to combust he gasped, '*Ah, mia rosa Inglesa.* Let's play a game.'

A game? A *game*? What was the man talking about? Why didn't he talk sense like normal people? 'Darn, I forgot my tennis racket.'

He didn't miss a beat, volleying her sarcasm right back at her. 'What a relief. You'd trounce my right-handed game.'

'So what is it you have in mind? I Spy?'

'I do spy the route your convoy and I were heading for before all this happened, the one to the nearest multinational peacekeeping camp.'

She snapped him an incredulous look. 'Why didn't you *say* so?'

'I *am* saying so, am I not?'

She exhaled in exasperation. But hope surged inside her, distracting her from the infuriating, disturbing man beside her, warding off exhaustion. She sat forward in her seat and pressed harder on the accelerator.

'We're a long way away,' he said. 'Let's park for the night.'

'You go to sleep, I'm not tired.'

'You're not *tired*, you're *finished*. You'll crash, and I'd rather you didn't do it literally. Anyway, it's me who must be awake to navigate this route and the avalanche paths intersecting it. Pull over.' His voice was firm. Final.

She had to concede. Pure adrenaline was keeping her going, and it would soon run out. Even if it didn't, she needed him awake to guide her. She followed his directions to a thick cluster of trees, turning the truck off once deep under their cover.

Deprived of sight in the absolute darkness, her other senses expanded and sharpened. And he filled them all to overflowing. His breathing, his heat, his scent—shouldn't he smell sweaty and repulsive? Then his touch joined the devastating mixture. His arm was going around her.

His *left* arm.

She tried to object, but he whispered in her ear, 'Let's keep the hard-earned warmth locked in, *piccola*. Now, settle down. Yes, like that, on my chest. This way I keep my arm elevated for optimum drainage and position of rest. Hmm, perfect. Now, if only we could have a hot drink and some music.'

She wanted to protest him moving his left arm at all, and his right arm to caress her. To laugh at him using her as a prop. To pinch him for wreaking havoc with her senses and thinking nothing of it. For behaving as if they were out camping!

But as she snuggled in the crook of his arm, nothing seemed to matter any more. He reclined fully, stretched out half beneath her, sandwiched her between his body and the back of the truck's seat and sighed. She settled on his heart and sighed too.

She really didn't think she'd fall asleep, but she did. Sank quick and deep into peaceful dreams. Just before she did, her mind crowded with the most ridiculous thoughts.

It felt like she was made to fit in Lorenzo's arms.

It felt like heaven.

If she didn't live to see another day, at least she now knew what *that* felt like…

'Come on, Sherazad. You can tell me!'

Lorenzo twirled a lock of her long hair around his fingers,

leaning forward to sniff it, sighing in appreciation. She snatched it from his bronzed fingers, only to yelp in distress when he—deliberately, she was sure—tangled them with hers. She jerked her hand away and glared at him.

Not that her chastising scowl had any effect. He continued his teasing, groaning in mock disappointment. 'You're not being fair. I told you *my* underwear size, favourite colour, material and style.'

She shot him another withering glance. 'Nobody asked you to supply those information gems!'

He retaliated with such a look of roguish entreaty, her heart skipped several beats. 'But I *did* supply them. It's only fair you reciprocate!'

'I'm *not* discussing my underwear with you!' She tried to sound scathing. Sadly, she came across like a scandalised Victorian. A scarlet one, she was sure. Sighing, she resigned herself to the fact that she'd never win a verbal match with him, and returned her eyes to the road where they belonged.

They'd been driving for nine hours in the pummelling rain, at the usual snail's-pace, on their third day on the road. She was certain they were lost in the zero visibility of the encroaching night. Long lost way before that.

And he was cheerfully continuing the outrageous Q and A game he'd invented!

They'd fallen into a pattern. They woke up at dawn, checked his shoulder which, to her immense relief, was healing at an almost alarming rate. They topped up his pain medication, then drove on and on, hiding—sometimes for hours—at any sign of life. That wasn't always possible with their huge truck. So far, thankfully, the people they'd come across were civilians. Some even waved to them. But when it was time to rest or sleep, they had to find well-camouflaged places to park in.

On their first dawn though, they had the added activity of arguing over splitting their limited food—her and her driver's leftover provisions.

Lorenzo insisted he had enough reserves in his body, not

like the spare sparrow that she was. She insisted that while she wasn't built like an ox, it wasn't her who had two litres of blood to reproduce. He hung a lactose bag in lieu of breakfast, and was furious when she drank the metallic-tasting tea but refused to eat the sandwiches.

Just when he looked ready to force-feed them to her, she remembered that they had a few crates of high-energy biscuits. Those were used in starvation scenarios and nine afforded an adult full nutritional support for a day. They ended up blowing another lock and crunching a few. Those had been their main sustenance ever since.

To keep them entertained, he played almost non-stop road games. She co-operated until his Q and A started trespassing on uncharted territory!

He was so blatantly enjoying her mortification, so clearly bent on embarrassing her, that she was almost tempted to burst his bubble. She bet he wouldn't be so smug if she told him it wasn't shocked prudence that was giving her palpitations. That it was the vision of him stripping down to those white silk boxers he had her fantasising about…

But no. That wouldn't be a good idea. He'd probably recover in a second and turn the tables on her.

'No underwear info?' he said lazily, interrupting her inner debate. 'OK, be that way. But if you won't tell me, can I guess?'

She barely caught back the provocative answer that sprang to her lips. She wasn't playing a game where he made the rules and held the winning hand. 'You can guess all you like! Don't expect confirmation of your accuracy, though.'

'Then if we're not swapping facts here, you don't mind if I fantasise?'

'As long as you don't share your juvenile fantasies, you're free to do as you please.' With that hopefully pithy and chastening remark, she concentrated on the road once more.

He was far from chastened.

He pretended baffled affront so well, anyone who didn't see the devils in his eyes would have bought his act. That was, until they heard what he said next. 'Not announce them? Not tell you, in detail, what I think would suit you most in the way of testosterone-provoking lingerie? What would be the point? Where would be the fun, the…pleasure?'

She wouldn't gulp, she told herself sternly. She wouldn't betray how his mouth-watering, intimate words were affecting her.

She gulped.

This audacity was only a foretaste. The main serving followed.

'If I were free in my fantasies, I'd have you in the same colour as your hair, that incredible amalgam of bronze, gold and silver—it's devastating with your flawless cream skin, by the way—in either opaque satin that cruelly cups and contours, or gossamer lace that barely hides and generously…hints. But I'd hesitate on the style. The scantiest amount of fabric, or something more concealing? While the first offers instant and sustained gratification, the second promises a steamy workout for the imagination. *Both* are equal hazards to the male blood pressure, though…'

He sighed at the vivid mental picture he'd painted, and she seriously considered yanking out his pain-relief catheter.

But he wasn't finished. 'As for size—'

'You stop your fantasising right there!'

'But I *have* stopped fantasising!' He blinked, looking genuinely taken aback. He fooled her for a split second, before he winked. 'Now I'm *estimating*. I'd say your cup size is—'

Her heat peaked. 'I can bite you again, you know.'

His tiger eyes flared mischief and…desire? 'Oh, please, do!'

Her foot slackened on the accelerator and the truck almost came to a stop. She knew he was just being the outrageous flirt—the practised, devastating philanderer—that he most certainly was. But she couldn't help her reaction. He made her feel wild, free…

No! She'd suffered even when she'd been cautious, so what if she were to be as reckless as this man tempted her to be? A man a hundred times as potent as all the men she'd known put together? She'd probably be destroyed…

She winced inwardly. What was with all the melodrama? Nothing had happened but a couple of kisses when they'd both been in shock and seeking solace. And there'd be no more. He hadn't touched her again in the past three days. Apart from sleeping in each other's arms, that was. The man was teasing her for laughs, to keep them from dwelling on their terrifying situation.

'Waiting for my punishment, *tesoro*!' His amused rumble coursed in her blood, making a mockery of her arguments. If he could do this to her when he was just having fun, what would he do to her if he actually put his mind to seducing her?

She was out of comebacks. He'd twist whatever she said to his advantage anyway.

Then he did something even more distressing. He leaned closer. 'You always promise what you don't deliver, Sherazad?'

That struck a nerve. 'Is this another question in your ridiculous Q and A? Or are you…?' She stopped. What was she saying? Now *she* was being ridiculous. There was no way he could have meant it the way she'd taken it.

He waited for her to continue, a puzzled look entering his eyes at her sudden burst of real irritation. When she remained silent, he relaxed again. 'What's ridiculous about underwear? I take underwear *very* seriously. But suit yourself. Would you rather I asked questions about ticklish spots, favourite positions…?'

A strangled sound burst from her and he guffawed. 'Favourite *sleeping* positions. Pick your mind up out of the gutter!'

'I will when your questions stop reeking of erotic innu-endo.'

'You mean you don't mind personal questions if they don't have sexual overtones?'

She minded. Any personal question at all. She was here to forget her personal life.

But she knew if she said she did, Lorenzo would find an even more embarrassing topic to corner her in. Let him ask his personal questions. She could always present him with her famed blank face.

She tossed him a challenging look. 'I don't mind—if you can keep your mind away from body parts long enough to formulate such a question.'

He made a theatrical gesture, putting the back of his hand across his forehead. 'I might do that only at the cost of a hefty chunk of my sanity. All right. For now!' She bristled at that last shot. He just had to have a last word, didn't he? 'So—why Sherazad?'

At last a question she could answer. One everyone she'd ever met asked. 'Ah, my name! Simple really. My mother is part Turkish. All lovely olive skin, dark hair and curves. She always thought her name, Rose, a gross misnomer, and swore she'd give her daughter an exotic name. She *swears* I was born dark. I'm not sure she's convinced yet I was just cyanosed after the eighteen-hour labour, and not switched by an evil plot at the neonatal ward...'

Lorenzo's appreciative laugh sent thrills surging though her. Ignoring the silly fluttering, she went on, 'I was born bald, but as I had unmistakable black eyes, she thought my hair would sprout as black and I'd turn out the image of her Turkish grandmother. So she named me after her.'

'Then you shocked everyone by turning all cream and gold and elfin. But you retained the black eyes. The com-bination is...indescribable.' His tone was light. But his eyes weren't. Could it be he wasn't just obeying his male pro-gramming of flirting with the only female on hand? Could it be he was as attracted to her...?

She snapped her eyes back to the road, her breath clogging in her throat. After spending the last three nights in his arms, so to speak, her awareness of him was heightened to the point of pain. And he was making it harder to bear and impossible to ignore. She was still in shock at the very concept of finding a man attractive. She'd come to abhor the very idea of sex. But to find herself not only attracted to but lusting after a man, and a clearly consummate seducer at that...

It had to be the danger playing havoc with her senses! No matter what she thought, or what he said to the contrary.

A snide little voice inside her sniggered at her blatant self-deception.

She ignored that voice, changed the subject. 'Thank God we have spare diesel. Not that I think it'll be of much use. In this weather, with no sun or stars to navigate with, I'm afraid we're lost anyway.'

He came closer, too close. Then he put his cool, gentle lips to her throat, at the point where her blood surged just under her skin. The steering-wheel lurched in her hands.

'Your pulse is thundering.' And was there any question why? 'Don't be afraid, *piccola*.' His words vibrated in her flesh and her bones promptly melted. Did he think he was soothing her? That her heart was about to crash out of her chest with fear? 'We're not lost and I swear I *will* take you to safety.'

She jerked a nod and he withdrew with a lingering caress to her cheek. 'As for the weather, remind me to write Mother Nature a letter of thanks. It seems all hostile entities are hiding from her wrath. Anyway, I'm certain where we're heading, and I'd say we'll be there some time tomorrow. So relax.'

Relax? Yeah. Right.

He continued teasing her, interrogating her, acting the tour guide. But it was his demonstrative sensuality that was driving her crazy. In every way. When the temptation to stop the truck and throw herself in his arms grew too ridiculous, she resorted to attacking him.

'It must be nice belonging to a race of indiscriminate sexual sportsmen, huh?'

He just smiled crookedly and retaliated. 'Much better, and much more fun, than belonging to a race of hypocritical sexual repressionists.'

Her jab might have slid right off him, but his hurt. She'd heard *that* accusation too many times, until it had come to define her shortcomings, and her.

Then he turned her inside out again. 'But you must be a non-paying member of said race, *innamorata*. You may be reluctant on the...verbal front, but those eyes say everything. And when you kiss—I could have easily vapourlocked. Your repression is either missing or deactivated. *Do* try to access it, for both our sakes.'

Even after such cautionary remarks, when it was time to park for the night, they again sought each other's embrace with open eagerness. Among all his sensual fooling around, his stated motives were heat preservation and comfort. She added seeking sanctuary to hers. The voice inside her said she'd fabricate any excuse to be in his arms.

During the night, unable to fall asleep but secure that he was, she sought a more comfortable if far more intimate position. And she felt him. Hard.

She'd wondered if he hadn't tried anything in the last three nights because he was too depleted. He evidently wasn't.

She involuntarily squirmed against him and felt his arousal growing, his breathing quickening. Oh, lord. He'd interpret her movements as an invitation. She held her breath, scared out of her wits that he'd take her up on it. She wanted—yet she couldn't— What would she do if he...?

But he didn't even move. She gradually relaxed *and* tensed, until she lay quivering in amazed, answering passion, the proof that he could check his lust filling her with feelings she'd never known with another man.

Trust. Respect. Maybe the beginnings of something more…?

No. Nothing more. Never anything more.

They reached the multinational peace-keeping force's camp checkpoint next evening at eight p.m.

Since only she had identification papers, it was some time before MPKF command verified Lorenzo's identity. As usual, Lorenzo took the inconvenience in his stride and made use of the time as their truck was searched to continue her frontline education.

'I've only been to Central Camp,' he said, 'but I'd say they're all built to the same specifications, the best in camp systems, having all shelter and comfort requirements.' He glanced over to the sentries manning the checkpoint. 'Isn't that so?'

The four soldiers eyed him uneasily, still not sure if they could be friendly. Suddenly Lorenzo narrowed his eyes at one of them. *'Ehi! Siete Italiani, non siete?'*

The young soldier eagerly nodded, instantly forgetting his reticence, and for the next ten minutes he and Lorenzo drowned all present in a torrent of non-stop Italian. Only when they were finally OK'd to go ahead did Lorenzo deem it necessary to include some subtitles.

'Paolo said there are almost four thousand people here, mostly military troops, but about ten per cent are the personnel responsible for the camp's deployment, maintenance, services and coordination. Not to mention the medical staff.'

'That's *all* he said? Does every word in English translate to a thousand in Italian?' she teased. 'And *Paolo*? Whatever happened to military discipline?'

'We're both Florentines, *piccola*! Practically brothers.' He shook his expressive hand, fingers grouped together in the characteristic Italian gesture, his eyes gleaming with clear national pride. 'Exchanging our entire family histories is as mandatory to us as "How do you do?" is to you.'

Her eyes rounded in incredulity, and he chuckled. 'He did squeeze in some information about the camp. It's made of a weatherproof, prepared-for-heating/air-conditioning inflatable tentage system. Very handy in erecting and packaging. He said they put the whole camp up in ten hours. It also incorporates a field hospital.'

By now they were near enough for her to see the details of the camp. In a huge clearing strategically obscured by the surrounding mountain, there were dozens of neat rows of interconnected tents, each about four by six metres, which she assumed were the soldiers' and personnel accommodation. Lorenzo informed her that the independent ones in different sizes at the periphery of the camp were for the generators and water pumps, the ones in the centre were the camp's command offices and quarters, and the huge tents the mess hall and the hospital. Dozens of army and supply vehicles flanked the camp.

French Colonel Jean-Luc LaCroix, the camp's commander, welcomed them inside his tent, seated them and immediately ordered food, fresh clothes and quarters to be prepared for them.

The tall, wiry man looked tough and weathered and, from the multitude of frown lines all over his shrewd face, not given to smiling. But he was smiling now, his smile all for Lorenzo.

'It's incredible!' He patted Lorenzo on the back once more before he came to sit before him. 'We despaired of even news of you,' he said in heavily accented but proper English. 'But for you to escape, to cross the land, injured and all—incredible!'

Sherazad opened her mouth to correct his assumption about Lorenzo's injury, but Lorenzo shot her a silencing glance.

'I owe my escape to their disorganisation and predictability,' Lorenzo said. 'Afterwards, I exchanged medical advice and services for food and the occasional ride. Some asked for nothing in return, but those who did ask, those who reported me—I can't blame them. What they have to do to survive is beyond nightmarish.'

Colonel LaCroix nodded, his face settling back into its natural grimness. 'And it will get worse before it gets better. Peace treaties are being smashed left and right, and we're cornered into employing considerable force to stabilise the situation and minimise the suffering of non-combatants.'

The colonel paused, then that difficult smile emerged again. 'But at least we have you back. Tomorrow we escort you to your command. You're badly needed there. Now you must be checked by our battalion doctors.'

Lorenzo shook his head. 'There's no need. Dr Dawson took excellent care of me.'

Colonel LaCroix seemed to remember her presence, and turned to her with a sour grimace which she assumed was an apologetic smile. 'Dr Dawson, I deeply regret your convoy's destruction. We had no intelligence of the attack, and our forces were engaged deflecting raids. But I assure you, those responsible for your mission's untimely deployment will be held accountable. And those responsible for its destruction will be brought to international justice. Every effort is being done to retrieve those not accounted for among the…dead.'

Sherazad felt the blood rush to her head. She had no words to express how little she cared who got reprimanded for their role in that catastrophe. No words to express her anger that efforts to find the offenders would prove as ineffective as those employed to find Lorenzo.

Lorenzo must have felt her about to find those words, that they were about to burst out of her as brutal truths, for he rose, his gentle grasp compelling her up, and into silence. Then he said calmly, 'We'd like to call our people now, Colonel.'

The colonel extended his hand in invitation at once. 'Of course. Use my phone.'

Soon she was talking to her frantic family. They'd heard nothing but evasive reports about her fate for the past five days, and now nothing she said reassured them. She finally had to end the conversation with an adamant refusal to cut short her contracted time on the frontline, among her mother's tears and her father's agonised anger.

After the emotionally draining phone call, she clung to Lorenzo's supportive hand gratefully as they were escorted to a tent in the dormitory area.

It looked much the same as the other tents, but it was a stand-alone. Inside, the neon-lighted tent was state of the art, with its immaculate twin bunks and insulated flooring. But it was the hard-wall door and the tiny attached bathroom stall that made her guess it was one of the camp's luxury suites.

Just as Colonel LaCroix turned to leave, he stopped and said, 'We have female soldiers and personnel in the camp, Dr Dawson. I can arrange for a bed with one of them.'

And leave Lorenzo? was the first thought that screamed in her mind.

Isn't it wiser—*safer*—to do so? the voice of reason whispered.

But what if he needed her? What if, now he'd got her to safety as he'd promised, he collapsed? Even if he didn't, she *couldn't* leave him. Wiser and safer be damned.

She instinctively backed into his hard body, seeking to protect him, seeking his protection.

He immediately accommodated her body and her needs, answering for her. 'Everything's just fine, Colonel.'

As the Colonel left and she sagged against Lorenzo, felt him warm and tough and overwhelming, she knew.

Everything was *not* just fine.

CHAPTER FOUR

'YOU—*fool*!' Lorenzo accused his reflection.

Exhaling heavily, he escaped its harsh glare, lowered his head to the basin and splashed his face with water as hot as he could bear.

It was nothing compared to the heat roiling in his gut.

He raised his eyes again and met the diabolical-looking stranger's in the small mirror. Grimacing, he reached for the packaged shaving kit and set about changing his appearance back to normal.

Once he'd removed the most glaring sign of his two months on the run, he stared at his haggard and almost forgotten self.

What had come over him to accept this sleeping arrangement?

Accept? Now, that had to be one of the greatest jokes of the century. He'd jumped at the opportunity. He'd nearly grabbed Sherazad when the colonel had suggested taking her away. He'd even contemplated shoving the man out.

But he *had* only been responding to Sherazad's unspoken appeal. She had backed into him—had seemed scared at the idea of leaving him.

He exhaled an exasperated, low laugh at his flimsy defences.

Of course she had! They knew nothing about each other—apart from what their instincts told them, and the basics of names, occupation and underwear colour—but their shared ordeal had created a bond between them, like that between comrades-in-arms.

But he was the veteran and she the rookie. He took it in his stride; she was traumatised. To her, even this sanctuary

53

was full of strangers. She needed to cling to her only familiar anchor in this nightmare. And he'd taken advantage
of that need.

He'd done it not because he was accommodating her or
because she was now a part of his team. He just couldn't
bear letting her out of his sight. He not only wanted her
safe, he wanted to keep her safe himself.

He wanted her—full stop.

But no matter what he wanted, he shouldn't have given
in to her anxiety and his desires. Their desperate situation
had ended, and life-affirming intimacies were no longer
needed to sustain their spirits and sanity. He didn't have to
remain this close to her. He'd better not.

But he had.

And there she was, out there. Showered, fresh, warm.

In bed.

Oh, God, he prayed. *Let her be asleep when I get out.*

She wasn't.

She was sitting up, knees drawn up beneath her chin, her
eyes wide and bottomless with turbulent emotions.

He should be at the point of collapse. He should look at
her and see yet another desirable woman whom he could
just as easily take or leave. What should be and what was
were poles apart.

The pounding desire that seemed to have become his natural state erupted into something he had no experience with,
no defences against. His every muscle quivered with the
effort not to pounce on her. It was only post-traumatic stress
intensifying their attraction, he reiterated to himself. Now
they knew there *would* be a tomorrow, they had to think
about it.

He couldn't think about tomorrow.

All he could think of was her. Them. Together. Now.

He stumbled two steps towards her, then stopped. She
cried out. *'Lorenzo!'* What was that hot, volatile emotion in
her cry? Confusion? Apprehension?

Frustration?

He could swear it was the latter—could swear he heard his mind buckling. He stumbled the rest of the way to her.

There was no tentative exploration this time. This time he didn't just need to touch her, soothe her; this time he needed to devour her. Hot, raging hunger roared inside him, bordering on madness. He bore down on her with his full weight, his lips opening on her yielding mouth, his tongue invading her moist heat with a sensual ferocity he'd never experienced. The triumph, the sheer clawing pleasure of possession spread through him. Then he heard a strange noise, almost a snarl—coming from him?

The predatory sounds shocked him. Must have shocked her too. She made a frantic sound and he jerked his head back. She looked petrified.

He'd scared her.

He'd scared himself.

He'd never even imagined losing control, never imagined how liberating it would feel—how potentially disastrous. He tried to move off her, but his body was not his to command. *'Tesoro…'*

'I—I know I invited this—did this to you…' Her wide, wild eyes went to his huge arousal pressing into her thighs through their army-issue pyjamas, before snapping back to his face. 'But…if I ask you to stop…'

He stared at her. Somehow—and he didn't know how he knew it—that choking fear in her voice, that twist of revulsion to her lips, were not a reaction to him as much as to a memory—a conditioning. What had happened to her? Had she once sought comfort in a man's arms as she'd done now, and he wouldn't stop, even when she'd asked him to?

No! He was letting his imagination go wild. She'd just changed her mind. As she was entitled to.

'Tesoro, you only have to stop kissing me and I'd stop too.' He wrung a smile from his aching lips, stroking her glossy hair off her forehead gently, his hand almost patting her instead with its trembling.

'Really? Even when you're *that*…' She blushed again as her smouldering eyes sought out his straining manhood.

He felt their gaze there, more tormenting than any caress. He tried to laugh, but he was too distressed to pull it off. 'I *did* stop, if you haven't noticed.'

Her eyes widened as if she'd just realised that. Then something warm and satisfied crept into them until they became slumberous once more. She relaxed in a boneless, unconsciously provocative pose. 'I was only asking if you *would* stop, not asking you to.'

He groaned again and braced himself against her reason-annihilating whispers and sight. '*Tesoro*, I may be Superman, but you're kryptonite. If you think you'll want me to stop again—'

'I won't.'

Her tremulous promise shuddered through him. Yet he waited for her to make the first move. She made it, and he wasn't prepared for the flare of lust her soft touch on his cheek ignited. Then her fingers snaked into his hair, tugging at him until he sank into her surrendering, demanding kiss.

This time, he'd go slow, he promised himself. And he tried, but she was answering his unhurried passion with maddening, maddened moans. They spread like wildfire in his system, scorching his control.

She opened her mouth fully, surrendering to his invasion, inviting it. She arched her supple back off the hard mattress and offered her softness to his hardness instead, squashing herself against him, as if trying to get under his skin, mix with his flesh. Feeling her body without the bulky thermal clothes they'd been smothered in was almost too much to bear.

No, not almost. *Too much.*

He tore his lips away from hers. His heart was bursting, his lungs about to explode, his senses stampeding. She cried out and clung to him. Her hot, moist lips grabbed at any part of him, her teeth biting an anchor so he wouldn't slip away.

'I'm not going anywhere,' he growled as a perfect sharp tooth grazed his tough skin. The pain-pleasure nearly drove him over the edge. 'I'll blow an artery if I don't…*see* you— touch, taste all of you. *Now!*'

'Yes, yes…' Her voice was cracked and deep, her irises glazed.

His hands didn't know where to start. They wanted to tear her out of her clothes all at once. They roamed her in an indecisive frenzy until she pressed them to her breasts and whimpered again, 'Lorenzo, *please*…'

Of course. How could he have thought to start anywhere else?

But his hands were no longer the ultra-dexterous tools he'd grown to depend on. They fumbled with the shapeless, drab beige pyjamas, finding it hard to even work the buttons. He finally opened her top with all the finesse of a deprived child tearing open his first birthday present. He pounced on her breasts with rough hands and watering mouth. His senses overloaded with their texture and resilience, their scent and taste. His mind filled with her cries, and images of taking every liberty he'd never even imagined with her.

He squeezed his eyes shut and prayed for control. Her earlier evident fear of a man's lust clawed at him. She'd be horrified if she knew what he wanted to do with her. He opened his eyes and met her delirious ones.

No, she wouldn't. He could read it in her vacant gaze, hear it in her muttered incoherencies. She'd ceased to be Sherazad. She'd become a mass of cravings, seeking life affirmation at the expense of everything else.

This *was* post-traumatic stress.

The certainty swatted him back from the edge. Stopped him from closing his lips and teeth over her turgid flesh and sinking into her, thrusting them both to the release they were going crazy for.

But how he wanted to—wanted *her*.

He'd only ever wanted one thing with the same ferocity: to remain alive, to not have it end at those monsters' hands.

But it was wrong. For every reason there was, he should leave her alone. He must.

But how could he leave her in this condition? He needed to pleasure her more than he needed his own pleasure. Yet giving her release still meant he'd begun a sexual relationship with her, taken advantage of her in her moment of utmost vulnerability. So far, it had only been a few frenzied kisses and partial nudity. Any further and the damage to their relationship would be irretrievable.

He could think of only one way out of this.

'I was right.' His attempted laugh came out a ragged groan.

Her dazed eyes tried to focus on him. 'Wha—?'

'About the size!' He saw her eyes go blank, then slowly widen with comprehension. 'I couldn't have imagined the shape, though. You're beyond my fantasies. And strike all those about underwear too. Without any is definitely what suits you most.'

She stared at him for a few heart-bursting moments. He waited for anger, affront to fill her eyes. Instead, they emptied of all expression. Letting out a sobbing exhalation, she pulled her top together in shaky movements.

Once again, as if they'd both agreed, they pulled apart. She slumped back on her bed and he staggered to his.

They had to work together, he railed at himself over the roaring, tearing throb of frustration. And not in a nice, safe metropolitan hospital. They had to stay sharp, impartial and unencumbered. Even if he had on occasion indulged in purely sexual liaisons with co-workers, it wouldn't be the same with her. He was certain she didn't indulge in blowing-off-steam sex. He didn't feel the uncomplicated lust for her that had long been his only response to women. Even if she were and he did, he didn't want post-traumatic sex, not with her. Last but not least, she was on the frontline temporarily. He was there for life.

End of story.

All that remained was to end it on a light note.

When the pain in his loins eased enough for him to breathe, he turned to her. His smile was still a grimace. 'And while no bra is definitely you, no protection is definitely not me.'

Sherazad stared at his clean-shaven beauty and felt about to shatter with wanting him. With wanting to correct him.

She *was* protected. *And* safe. She was certain he was too.

He was safe in every way. His restraint astounded her. That and his ability to distance himself and handle any situation lightly proved she had nothing to fear from him. The knowledge had been there, on an instinctive level, from the start. She *had* trusted him with her life, against all evidence.

But was that trust enough to have her writhing in a mindless sexual frenzy, begging him to take her? Whatever had happened to her revulsion and painful inhibitions?

Apparently gone, to be replaced by an almost frightening craving for him. A craving that could no longer be explained away as a survival mechanism. And if she was honest, it couldn't be excused by post-traumatic stress either. She just wanted him.

She had planned on using her frontline experience for psychological rehabilitation, but she couldn't use him for sexual therapy—could she?

As if it was up to her! It was clear he considered this a mistake he didn't want to compound by going all the way. Though it surprised her, she couldn't and didn't want to dwell on his reasons. What mattered was that he wanted to end the crisis with a return to their teasing ease.

She agreed with him. No matter how it disappointed her, it was better this way.

So she joined his game, arching one eyebrow at him. 'If you can't find ''protection'' in a military installation, Dr Banducci, where can you find it?'

Surprise rippled across his amazing face. But only for a second. As usual he picked up the teasing and hurled it back at her multiplied.

'Shall I announce my…pressing need for a generous supply on the camp's PA system?'

She'd started it, but it didn't mean she could sustain it. She knew she must look like fresh liver, imagining the extended love-making sessions he alluded to.

She'd never had those. Or *love-making* for that matter. But with Lorenzo…

What? she asked herself in exasperation. What would it be like with Lorenzo? He could easily turn out to be another Jack. Jack had seemed in control at first too.

It was better to cling to that possibility.

At her blushing silence he exhaled, his face losing its devil-may-care façade. 'Let's sleep, Sherazad. We'll need our stamina for the coming ordeals.'

The ordeals started much earlier than expected. The professional ones at least.

A wailing siren snapped Sherazad out of her troubled sleep. She spilled out of bed onto wobbling legs and bumped into an equally alarmed Lorenzo.

'A raid?' she asked, her throat thick and her voice rasping.

'No.' His voice was crisp and certain. 'Incoming casualties. Let's go.'

He turned his back as she jumped into her clothes, and she was almost thankful for the brain-splitting sirens and her freezing hands. They, along with what remained of her fast-evaporating inhibitions, stopped her from running her hands down that expanse of bronze-packaged sinew and muscle. And the emergency, of course. Lord, the emergency!

She must still be partially asleep if she was drooling over him now.

But as he started buttoning up his shirt, she had to stop him.

'A topping-up in pain medication is in order,' she said, flustered by the sensual flare in his eyes, remembering her cat-in-heat state last night. 'You say you don't need it but, as your doctor, I say you do. No telling what you'll need your arm for today.'

She finished injecting the analgesic as she spoke, adjusted his bandages, then helped ease his arm into his jacket sleeve. As she stepped away, he caught her back and pressed her to him for one intense, precious second. *'Grazie, tesoro.'*

Then they ran out.

'Bear in mind that doctors here are military personnel,' he said as they approached the field hospital from the personnel entrance. 'And stay with me at all times.'

'Being the boss already?' she gasped as she tried to keep up with his far longer stride.

He gave her a tight grin. 'You bet.'

Then they arrived to find the triage area a scene of mayhem.

The area was huge, but incoming casualties seemed endless. Patient stations consisting of litters placed on sawhorse frames were overflowing, with each of the medical personnel tending three or four patients at once. Shouted orders and yelled reports in many languages mingled in an ear-splitting cacophony with screams of pain and despair.

'Stretched,' was Lorenzo's grim assessment. 'They're not the main combat hospital in the region, just a field division. The situation must have called for immediate medical action before evacuation. But at least they're well equipped.' He flicked a nod at the shelving along the tent sides. They were filled with consumable supplies, from IV fluids and administration sets to drugs and dressings to evaluation forms and identification tags. There was an overhead rail from which IV solutions and blood were suspended. 'Let's see what we can do.'

Lorenzo caught hold of a nurse and demanded to be taken to his triage officer, who was inundated. At Lorenzo's appearance a desperate look lit the younger man's pale blue eyes.

'Dr Banducci?' he asked in patent relief. 'Lieutenant Sjorgen, Chief of Surgery. Are you well enough to help?'

Lorenzo gave an emphatic nod. 'Status?'

'Surface-to-surface missiles hit their outpost, followed by a blitz. They were temporarily stationed in an abandoned office building in the most contested area in the region. We have all sorts of ballistic, blast and burn injuries. Casualties barely removed from the rubble and out of line of fire, with hardly any primary measures applied on the way. Six fatalities, thirty-nine critical, forty-eight varying ambulatory, and that was the field paramedics' estimates twenty minutes ago. More incoming.'

'Chemical, biological or radiation contamination?' Lorenzo bit off the question.

'Assorted white phosphorous burns from explosives. Phosphorus deactivated with water-soaked dressings.'

'Everyone triaged?'

'Just half the critical number so far.'

'Is it OK if I triage the other half?'

'It's more than OK,' Lt Sjorgen said fervently. 'In fact, being the one with superior experience among us, you should be the triage officer.'

'But you know your facility's resources.' Lorenzo didn't deny Lt Sjorgen's assessment of their relative expertise. 'Only you can assess the facility's ability to sustain momentum and orchestrate evacuation. Give me two doctors and four nurses. Dr Dawson and I will perform triage and direct resuscitation, while you manage your resources, direct the preoperative holding area and the movement into the operating room.'

'We'll need you in Theatre too, Dr Banducci,' Lt Sjorgen said. 'I don't have enough senior surgeons to handle even the cases I triaged. Most of them won't withstand evacuation to Central.'

'I'll wrap up here and follow through in Theatre,' Lorenzo said.

With a terse nod, it was agreed.

As they ran to their patients, the required personnel already at their elbows, Sherazad allowed herself an overwhelmed internal second. At the magnitude of disaster. At Lorenzo's influence and resourcefulness.

It was amazing seeing him in action. In minutes, he triaged thirty casualties and determined priorities, not pausing to puzzle over any sign, seeming to know the diagnoses as if by second sight. He was assigning the last chores to his assistants when Head Nurse François Dupont called out to him to come take a look at the casualty he was already tending.

As they snapped on fresh gloves, Lorenzo growled orders for a list of items to be at their fingertips. A nurse rushed to do his bidding.

'Mechanism of injury?' Lorenzo bit off, taking in the soldier's appearance.

'The paramedics aren't sure,' François said. 'Blast injury, most probably.'

'Unconscious in the field?'

'No, Sergeant McFadden's GCS was 15 then. He deteriorated just as you came in. His breathing became 65, very shallow tidal volume. Pulse plunged down to 35, BP to 70 over 50, GCS to 3. I intubated and applied positive pressure ventilation. No venous access or exposure.'

'It's arterial gas embolism,' Lorenzo barked. 'Stop PPV and switch to high-flow supplemental oxygen with tight mask. Transfer him to a bed and lower its head as far as it will go—*now*!'

As François rushed to implement his orders, Sherazad's mind raced. She knew gas embolism with a blast injury meant that the shock wave had forced air from his lungs into his bloodstream. The air bubbles acted like clots, causing all sorts of neurological and cardiac complications, possibly culminating in a fatal myocardial infarction or stroke in a matter of minutes. His quickly deteriorating Glasgow coma scale, or GCS evaluation, measuring his degree of consciousness and responsiveness, indicated he was developing the latter.

She also knew that Lorenzo's decision to stop positive pressure ventilation was valid. PPV was life-saving for a casualty in respiratory distress, but in gas embolism it would only push more air into the circulation, complicating an already disastrous situation.

But she wondered about his decision to lower the casualty's head. She had to ask. 'Shouldn't we place him in the coma position, rather than the Trendlenburg position?'

She knew that placing Sgt McFadden with his left side down, his right elbow and knee supporting his body and his head at the same level as his heart placed his coronary arteries and head in their lowest position to protect against coronary and cerebral AGE. The head-down technique was no longer considered the position of choice.

Lorenzo nodded. 'Ideally, we should. But then we can't continue examining him in that position, and I doubt AGE is the worst of his injuries.'

She hadn't thought of that!

'Do you have a hyperbaric oxygen chamber?' Lorenzo asked the tall, blond nurse. He meant the chamber where oxygen was delivered at a pressure more than that of atmospheric pressure, dissolving the air bubbles into the blood again, with the pressure decreased gradually to keep it that way.

'Yes,' François answered. 'Do you want to transfer him there now?'

Lorenzo shook his head. 'Continue your report.'

François nodded. 'Suspected transected femoral artery. Haemorrhage controlled by direct compression. No other outward gross sign of injury.'

Lorenzo examined the injured leg, palpating the pulse in the foot. 'Distal pulse weak but felt,' he said. 'The artery isn't fully severed, then.' He inspected the bandage at the top of the thigh. Sherazad knew he'd remove it only when he was ready to perform definitive vascular, or artery, repair.

Right now it was the only thing stopping exsanguination, massive haemorrhage and rapid death. 'Compression pad effective.'

'But soaked,' Sherazad said as she gained high central venous access, slipping a large-bore catheter into the internal jugular vein.

Lorenzo frowned. 'It can't hold more than 250 ccs of blood. His stage three shock means he has another massive source of bleeding.'

'Chest? Abdomen? Pelvis?' Sherazad asked as she slipped the needle out.

'Could be any or all,' Lorenzo said. 'François—six units warmed type O, low-Rh titre blood. Full exposure—now.'

Once the ABCs of resuscitation were finished, they inspected Sgt McFadden from head to toe.

'Bilateral ruptured eardrums and air embolism indicate proximity to detonation epicentre…' Lorenzo murmured, as if thinking out loud. 'And high probability of other primary blast injuries. This close to the blast wave, the air in his gas-filled organs—lungs, stomach, small and large intestines—would have been so severely compressed, he probably ruptured at least one of them. His respiratory distress does suggest pulmonary contusion from the barotrauma. The secondary blast injury—from shrapnel propelled by the blast—accounts for his arterial injury…'

Sherazad was feeling the abdomen and listening with her stethoscope. She took it off for a second and said, 'His suspected internal damage and haemorrhage might also be caused by the tertiary blast injury, when the blast wave threw him against a solid surface. External contusions are suggestive.'

Lorenzo only nodded as listened to the chest. 'Absent breath sounds bilaterally, stony dull on percussion. Massive bilateral tension pneumothorax.'

So air *was* leaking out of his lungs, getting trapped in their covering, building up a pressure that collapsed them.

This was a rapidly fatal condition. As if it wasn't enough, she reported her own ominous findings.

'Abdomen distended, rigid, no bowel sounds.' That probably meant free blood in the abdomen, maybe inflammation of the membrane covering the organs from the spilled contents of the bowels. 'Haemoperitoneum? Maybe even acute peritonitis?'

'Shock with bradycardia supports it,' Lorenzo agreed. Shock with haemorrhage was always accompanied by tachycardia—increased heart rate. But when it was decreased, it suggested associated peritonitis.

She took her hands off Sgt McFadden's pelvic bones after examining them for stability. 'At least there are no signs of a pelvic fracture.'

'We have that to celebrate.' Lorenzo shot her a brief glance. 'Decompress the pleural space and stomach while I catheterise the urethra and perform a rectal exam.'

She finished the double needle thoracostomy, releasing the building air in the chest, then slipped in the nasogastric tube and attached it to a suction device. Both Lorenzo's catheter and his rectal exam yielded blood, supporting the diagnosis of ruptured bowels.

'We must operate to resuscitate here, not the other way around,' he said. 'He's not responding to transfusion as he's simply leaking the blood inside.'

'Will you do it?'

Before he could answer, incoming paramedics burst in with more casualties. Two were pronounced in terminal urgency.

Lorenzo bit off a few words to François to warm Sgt McFadden well on the way to Theatre, and to come back for him if no surgeon was available to perform the immediate laparotomy, the abdominal exploration. Then they raced over to the new casualties. At their sight, Sherazad froze in shock.

One of them was a woman.

Sherazad knew that women constituted a recognised percentage of armies today. She knew it shouldn't make a difference. It did. She rushed to her first.

So did Lorenzo. But after he'd subjected her to a lightning examination, he moved to the other soldier, who looked dead with a perforating chest wound.

Sherazad told herself he was checking the other casualty, but would return. He didn't. He didn't even relay his findings so she'd take necessary measures.

The woman was about her own age and build. Her pulse was thready, her BP non-recordable and her breathing a choked rattling. But she was conscious! Her eyes locked onto Sherazad's. The sheer terror in them bludgeoned her, paralysed her. The next second, those green eyes closed and the futile breathing and heartbeat stopped.

Sherazad jumped into CPR. She breathed into the woman's mouth but felt something blocking the airway. She snatched a laryngoscope and tried to investigate and remove the blockage. The woman had the most severe laryngeal fracture she'd ever seen!

'Leave her, Sherazad,' Lorenzo called out.

'I *won't*,' she cried as she reached for a suitable implement. In seconds she'd performed a tracheostomy, slicing an opening in the woman's trachea to bypass the blockage in her larynx, installed an endotracheal tube, grabbed a nurse and shouted, 'You—ventilate!' Then she swooped into cardiac compressions.

'I said leave her.' Lorenzo's call was harsher this time. 'Come give me a hand. This soldier's heart just stopped.'

'So did hers.'

'I *said*, come here!' he thundered.

She ignored him and kept on with her compressions. She darted feverish looks from her unresponsive patient to Lorenzo. He was intubating the soldier, starting him on PPV. Then he ordered the nurse to inject him with a muscle relaxant. She knew all this was in lieu of anaesthesia for emergency surgical intervention. Sure enough, he tore off the soldier's clothes and performed a left-sided thoracotomy to open the chest wall, an incision running from the breast-bone to the midaxillary line. Once he'd cut through the intercostals, the ribs' muscles, he separated the ribs with a rib-spreader and shouted, 'A Gigli saw.'

The moment he turned the electric saw on, it jerked in his weakened hand. He swore violently in Italian. 'Sherazad, you come *this second* and do this. Nurse—central venous access and warmed Ringer's lactate bolus—now!'

Casting a last desperate look at her lifeless patient, who was already being removed to make space for a still living casualty, she stumbled to Lorenzo's side, her whole being in uproar. She found control somehow and immediately used the saw to divide the sternum.

Then Lorenzo took over, moving the rib-spreader to the midline, exposing the chest organs, reaching deep into the soldier's chest and exploring the damage and bleeding sources. He worked at blinding speed, suturing the cardiac injury, the torn thoracic aorta and lung hilum, gaining control of the hemorrhage in under three minutes. Then he applied direct cardiac massage and the heart resumed beating. The casualty was rushed to Theatre for definitive repair and closure.

Before he followed his cases, he turned to her.

'You were out of line, Sherazad.' He sounded matter-of-fact, his very calmness pouring acid on her exposed nerves. 'You're new to all this, so I'll let it go—this once. But understand this—I am your triage officer, here and everywhere. Let me enlighten you what this means. It's my unfortunate lot to have total authority in triage decisions. In mass casualty situations we're bound by "logical categories". Critical injuries which have a high potential for survival are given *absolute* priority. Others, like your lady soldier, are considered unsalvageable, and we can't afford futile resuscitation efforts.'

'Who gave you the right to play God and decide who's salvageable and who isn't?' All her anguish came out in an eruption of fury. 'How do you know she wouldn't have responded with extended resuscitation?'

'I know because I've done this *hundreds* of times.' She felt his calm receding, saw it in his tautening face, heard it in his hardening voice. 'I know because I've learned the hardest way possible, trying to save everyone, and losing more people that way. This is triage at its most brutal, Sherazad. She had extensive crush injuries, not to mention a transected cervical spine—'

'She could have been in spinal shock—'

'A *transected* cervical spine!' He stressed his diagnosis forcefully. 'Total paralysis extending to her respiratory centre. Even if you'd obtained a pulse, she would've died minutes later, with the rest of her multi-system injuries. But then your preoccupation with her would have also killed the soldier who had a potentially lethal but, as you saw, controllable injury.'

By now she was shaking all over, shouting at the top of her lungs. 'Even if you're right, it's all because she was dragged away with a neck injury without as much as a hard collar. Those who ''rescued'' her are probably the ones who broke her neck!'

'You mean they should have risked getting shot, blasted or crushed by falling debris themselves, until they'd secured her cervical spine?' He shot her a disdainful glance as he strode away. 'This isn't a car accident setting, Sherazad. This isn't A and E. This is the frontline of a *war*. If you don't understand that, take the first flight home.'

CHAPTER FIVE

'ARE you still sulking?'

Sherazad did a double take as Lorenzo walked into their tent. She wasn't used to his shaven magnificence yet. His currently dishevelled, depleted, stubbled, but comparatively shaven magnificence.

'Don't you mean, am I still here?'

A tiny smile tugged at his tired lips. 'So you *are* sulking!'

She gave an indifferent shrug. 'I'd be too exhausted to sulk, even if I knew how to.'

His lips twitched. 'When was there ever a woman who didn't have sulking perfected into an art?'

'When was the last time you took your anti-chauvinism medication?'

He stared at her, his eyes crinkling slowly. Right along with her heart. Then he began to laugh, turning her to mush. She threw her pillow at his head. It only made him laugh harder.

'You're *definitely* sulking!' he guffawed triumphantly.

'I'm only angry you can keep such a sunny disposition after that—that—horrific day we just had!'

His sable eyebrows shot up, then descended heavily as his amusement ebbed. 'Sunny? Look again. I *am* delirious with exhaustion, though.'

'So why don't you go to sleep?'

'You mean, rather than harass you?'

She was ready to hurl his pillow as well when he suddenly yawned and rubbed his eyes, looking so very, very weary and so very…vulnerable. Almost defeated.

She thought a valve in her heart must have melted.

This melting was much more disturbing than the volcanic

sensual reaction she'd developed to his every look and sound and gesture. It involved more complex areas in her brain than those controlling her erogenous zones. She'd better find a distraction until this sappy moment of overwhelming tenderness passed. 'How did McFadden's operation go?'

This was one of the operations she hadn't witnessed. She'd joined Lorenzo in Theatre six hours ago, after all the casualties had been stabilised and moved on to the next echelon of medical care. That had been eight hours after he'd left her in Triage and he'd already looked awful. He'd denied he'd been in pain, of course, but she'd known he had been. She'd also known he wouldn't increase his pain relief for fear of compromising his hands' dexterity and power, his overall alertness.

He'd already performed ten operations of varying complexity, then performed six more in her presence. She'd acted as his first or second assistant, as the case warranted.

But she'd left before he'd wrapped up his last case, even when he'd asked her to wait for him. Not because she'd been sulking, but because she hadn't been able to put off running to the bathroom for one more second.

Now she purposely didn't ask about Corporal Delinski, the thoracotomy soldier. She was scared he'd tell her the corporal hadn't made it, that in the end she'd abandoned her patient for nothing.

'It was a mess.' Lorenzo threw himself on his bunk. The metal frame protested loudly and barely held up under his considerable weight. 'Operating with the table tilted for his gas embolism was a brand-new nightmare for me. And there were extensive bowel ruptures and abdominal cavity contamination…' He trailed off, rubbing his eyes vigorously with the heels of his hands, yawning and stretching like a tiger—even rumbling like one.

She insisted on ignoring the effect his sleepy exhaustion was having on her. 'So, did you do definitive repairs?'

He blinked at her with turbid honey eyes. It took him a

moment to process her question. 'No, no—I went for damage control surgery.'

She knew little about this multiple-trauma surgical approach. But she knew one thing. 'Isn't that controversial?'

'Not in my book.' He sat up a bit only to slump again. It alarmed her to see how sallow his bronze skin looked.

'Have you eaten?'

'They passed lunch over case number ten, but I decided not to drop crumbs and spill tea in my patient's pleural cavity!'

'You're joking, right?'

'What do you think?'

'Did I say you're impossible? You're way beyond that!'

He sighed complacently in the face of her wrath. 'I'm also way beyond hungry. And way beyond even holding a sandwich. Ah, for the days you gave me dinner intravenously.'

She huffed and made a sudden move to rise. He clung to her hand.

'Where are you going? Taking Colonel LaCroix's offer of female roommates?'

She shook off his hand. 'No! Going to see if I can schedule you for a sense-of-humour transplant. Get you a suppressant at least!' Then she walked out of the tent to the sound of his feeble yet very potent chuckling.

In minutes she returned with dinner, only to find him dozing. She placed the tray on the folding table and stood looking down at him.

Even after all he'd been through—the abduction, the two months on the run, the shooting and the days after it, not to mention today's ordeals—he still radiated something indomitable...

She picked up the bowl of soup, knelt beside him on the bunk and touched him gently. He started.

'Damage control surgery...' He jerked up to a sitting position, continuing the abandoned topic, the spaced-out look in his eyes telling her he was more than half-asleep. 'Is irreplaceable, in my opinion…'

'Soup!' She held the filled spoon to his lips. He obediently opened them and slurped noisily.

'Excuse me, *innamorata*. I remember I could close my mouth properly once.' He smiled sheepishly and attempted to drink with fewer sound effects. 'Hmm, hot food. I'd almost forgotten.'

'Why is it irreplaceable?' She was interested in learning about the surgery, but she needed the distraction more. Distraction from the scenario playing in her head. How, after she'd fed him, she'd strip him, bathe and dry him, push him back on his bunk, strip and plaster her flesh to…

Post-traumatic stress. It just had to be. What else could explain her metamorphosis from a frigid manhater into a nymphomaniac? But did a nymphomaniac lust only after one specific man?

She looked at him again. That sleepy, steamy look in his eyes, everything about him… Did she even have to wonder?

'Hot food *is* replaceable, regrettably.' He finished his soup and started rumbling his enjoyment deep in his chest at every piece of chicken she fed him. 'If only you knew the things I had to eat those couple of months. I won't tell you if you've just eaten, in the interests of keeping your meal down.'

Whatever she imagined he'd had to do to survive, reality must have been far harsher. She felt a fierce pang of thankfulness that he had survived, that he was here with her. 'You can tell me anything. I'm not in the least squeamish. And you know I was talking about damage control surgery.'

Lorenzo licked his lips, managing to look both wicked and innocent. 'I know no such thing. I'm asleep.'

Sherazad gave him a warning look and he raised a hand in surrender. He leaned back, his eyes shifting into a different focus as his mind changed gears to his professional side.

'I don't even consider other surgical approaches to multiple-trauma patients,' he said. 'The only concerns with them are haemorrhage control, abdominal contamination and further injury prevention. I achieved haemorrhage control by tying the abdominal aorta and packing the abdomen to apply direct pressure to the bleeding sources. I prevented abdominal contamination by stapling shut the ruptured intestines and washing out the peritoneum. Once I had a stable patient, prolonging dangerous anaesthesia time and adding the trauma of definitive repairs would have been criminally stupid. I even left him open.'

'Now, *that's* revolutionary!'

He gave her a chiding pout. 'Open, not exposed! I applied a vacuum pack over his abdominal contents—you know, that plastic seal?—and placed suction catheters to drain excess exudate and blood. Even if I hadn't intended to re-operate, I would have left him open to guard against abdominal compartment syndrome. You know what that is?'

She did know. 'A severe rise in intra-abdominal pressure after extensive abdominal trauma and exploration—especially when combined with packing to stop haemorrhage—that severely compromises cardiovascular, respiratory, renal and cerebral functions.'

His eyebrows rose in approval. A tingle of pleasure buzzed through her. She thought it best to ignore it. 'But how did you predict he'd develop it? Did his abdominal contents bulge above wound level? Was there resistance or tension when you tried to close the abdominal wall?'

'Those are the main indications, yes, but just the possibility that it would develop is indication enough, Sherazad. Trust me, you don't want a patient with ACS. The best treatment is definitely prevention. For now he's in Critical Care, getting stabilised so he can withstand further surgery rather than dead on table of intra-operative metabolic failure. Do you know what that is?'

She did, and felt very good about it. 'Failure of coagulation, hypothermia and metabolic acidosis, which would render haemorrhage control impossible. I guess with this rationalisation a surgeon who goes after definitive surgical repair would end up with a perfectly patched-up but dead patient.'

'*Perfetto, tesoro.*' He pinched her cheek softly, and she felt as absurdly pleased as she used to as a child when an idolised teacher applauded her efforts. 'Coming from a non-surgeon, that's remarkable. You really have the tenets of surgery down pat. I'm surprised you didn't want to be a surgeon. You have the knowledge and you have the hands.'

'You mean I'm so good I can stay?' She couldn't help trying to get her own back. He had kept his voice down when he'd reprimanded her, keeping it between them. But even if there'd been no witnesses to his harsh words, they were still stinging.

His face lost every trace of lightness. 'For all the people who need your skill and compassion here, I'd beg you to stay. It's you I'm worried about.'

Her heart kicked her ribs at his sudden intensity. His sudden sincerity. *Don't go there, Sherazad. Didn't you mistake Jack's intensity for sincerity too? And Jack was a two-dimensional creep, not like Lorenzo, that twisting, turning paradox!*

She laughed off his words. 'Sure didn't sound that way back there. You made me sound like a hazard to the sick and injured.'

'I was only saying I've been down that road before you.' He stopped her hand as she started breaking the bread in bite-sized pieces, enfolding it in his. 'The one paved with good intentions? I may have done it a bit too harshly…'

Her eyebrows shot up. '*May? A bit*?'

He inclined his head graciously. 'OK, I was too harsh.'

'You might have also been wrong!' Suddenly her anguish resurfaced and she glared her pent-up rage and denial at him.

He held her incensed glance for a long moment. Then he sighed. 'Is that what you truly think?' His awesome baritone and eyes filled with that empathy that had once had her crying rivers. It brought her close to that again. A tear escaped.

'It doesn't matter what I think. Nothing matters. She's dead.'

'It matters, Sherazad.' He wove his right hand into her hair, bringing her face closer to his. 'She may be dead, but there'll be hundreds of others to save, thousands of decisions to make and fulfil. If you think I was wrong, if you can challenge my decision, my rationale, then *prove* me wrong based on facts, not on emotional response, and I'd be the first to admit my mistake. Do everything in my power never to repeat it. I have no ego here, Sherazad. I only want to do the best thing possible for as many people as possible.'

She drew in a ragged breath, keeping her eyes averted. 'You weren't wrong.'

'You believe that?' he persisted. 'You agree with my decision?'

She raised rebellious eyes. 'This time.'

'Meaning you intend to question every one I make, eh?'

'Got any problems with that?' She puffed out her chest, raising both eyebrows in challenge. 'Or do you expect your team members to follow in your wake like sheep? If you do, say so now and I'll see about that plane home.'

His eyes fell to her breasts, and she sucked her chest back in hastily. The memory of her begging for his touch there deflated her bravado. That and the knowledge that she was being stupid. All through the day, Lorenzo had proved his reputation as a healer had been underestimated.

He was still staring down at her breasts and they responded obediently to his visual caress, growing heavy, nipples taut and aching. With what seemed like a great effort, he dragged glazed eyes up and exhaled. 'I'm sorry I said what I did, but it had to be said. Believe it or not, I only wanted to spare you…'

'Kind of you, I'm sure.' She stuffed a piece of buttered bread in his mouth, stopping his words. She could handle emotional or physical arousal individually. Combined, she had no chance. He took her hint and fell silent, concentrating on chewing and murmuring his pleasure as he surrendered to her ministrations.

With the last mouthful of cake he mumbled, 'Now, that's irreplaceable. Unprecedented, too. No one's ever fed me before.'

'What? Not even your mother?'

He shook his head. 'My mother was an unusual *donna Italiana*. She taught me self-sufficiency at two when my friends were spoon-fed until they were twenty-two. But maybe she wasn't unusual as much as she wasn't ready for me. When Piero was born, it was totally different—' He stopped abruptly, some dark emotion eclipsing his expressive features.

Suppressing it with a visible effort, he was back to his teasing self in seconds. 'Would it be too much if I asked you to brush my teeth?'

'This is a comprehensive service, *signore*.' She grinned, hiding her agitation at witnessing the bolt of torment on his face and her overwhelming curiosity at the reason behind it. Something to do with his brother. But what? Bitter rivalry? An irrevocable falling out? Alienation from his family? Family was all-important to Italians—was this why he'd abandoned his illustrious career to be on frontlines everywhere?

She gave up speculating. Until he chose to enlighten her, if he ever did, she'd only come up with guesses.

She tugged at him to take him to the bathroom, but she couldn't even budge him. His formidable body was as limp as when he'd been comatose.

'You weigh half a ton, right?'

'Right now?' he grumbled sleepily. 'That's a very conservative estimate. I wasn't planning on moving again this century. I was thinking you'd take my teeth for a good scrubbing…' Then he slumped back completely, his far superior weight pulling her off her feet towards him.

It wasn't the impact of landing on him that knocked the

breath out of her or prevented her from drawing another. It was having her breasts crushed against his hard chest, her legs splaying around his hips, her lips landing on his warm throat…

He didn't seem to mind at all. He only turned around, taking her with him, wrapping himself around her, imprisoning her between his legs and the tent wall, mumbling, '*Mmm—il cielo sulla terra…*' and promptly falling asleep.

Heaven on earth.

That was what he'd said. And in the middle of this hell on earth, being in his arms, whether for survival, in madness or by accident, surely was.

She was getting used to this—getting to crave this. Getting to *depend* on this. It scared the hell out of her. Far more than the raging war around her did.

She'd survived a personal war and a nearly fatal battle. She doubted she'd survive Lorenzo…

Sherazad had slept in his arms.

She'd let him hug her all night and shared the comforts of her generous spirit and warm body with him.

Now Lorenzo didn't dare shift one aching muscle. She'd wake up if he did. Then she'd move away. He couldn't bear that.

Just one more hour like this. He needed just one more hour. Then he'd let her go. Once he did, he'd never hold her again.

The next second she opened her eyes. And looked directly into his soul.

No! He *needed* his one more hour.

But if he couldn't have it, he'd have one more kiss.

He traced the line of her flushed, tender lips with his left thumb and rose on his sound elbow to fill his eyes with the achingly lovely sight of her in his arms.

'*Buon giorno, mia bella,*' he whispered, caressing her elegant cheekbone, before returning to her lips, dipping his forefinger between them, coaxing them apart. 'Thank you for last night.'

He watched the inky depths of her eyes flare. Was it welcome? The eager invitation he craved—and dreaded? Didn't she know what a look like that would do to him? Didn't she have any mercy? He found the words rushing out in his native language.

She giggled. 'I said I understand the odd Italian *word*. I found it nowhere in that speech.'

'Doesn't matter, as long as you understand this.' He took her lips and she sighed and opened them to receive him. And if he had any sanity left, her hungry tenderness made sure he lost it.

He absorbed all he could of her, gradually sinking into something far more consuming. She followed him, flowed into him. His tongue mated luxuriously with hers, mingling their moans of pleasure, his hands roving over her. Her small, hot body rewarded his patient hunger with undulations of mute need. He'd needed a kiss. Now he needed all of her, his surging body already thrusting against her softness to the tempo of their pounding hearts...

Another pounding intruded on their sensual cocoon. He had no idea how long it had been gnawing away at his consciousness before it had registered.

He jerked away from her, feeling like he'd peeled off his skin.

'I don't know if I'll kiss or kill whoever it is!'

Lorenzo heaved himself up from the bunk, leaving her to scramble to her feet, adjusting her clothes in mortification.

So he considered kissing their interrupter! That told her a lot. He believed this last episode of madness had been another mistake, thankfully aborted. Well, it seemed she couldn't pass a day without committing some gigantic error. What was one more?

It was Lt Sjorgen at the door. He apologised profusely for disturbing them, but still walked in without waiting for an invitation.

'Definitely no kissing,' Lorenzo whispered to her as he followed him. 'Seriously contemplating killing, though.'

She grimaced at him, sure she was red enough to flood the tent in a rosy glow. Not that Lt Sjorgen gave any indication he noticed anything as he sat on her still made-up bunk. Lorenzo gently pressed her down on his own dishevelled bunk and sat beside her.

The lieutenant got to the point of his early morning call at once. 'Dr Dawson, Dr Banducci, we can't thank you enough for your efforts yesterday. We would have lost so many more people if it hadn't been for you. But now we have a favour to ask of you. We know you must be eager to get back to your operation, but we hoped you could follow up your cases.'

Lorenzo seemed surprised that they'd assumed he wouldn't. 'I never leave my patients unfollowed-up except if it's beyond my physical ability. I intend to stay here until they're all on the sure way to recovery.'

'That's the problem, Dr Banducci. *They* won't stay here.'

Lorenzo's face suddenly became an aggressive mask. 'Sergeant McFadden and Corporal Delinski *can't* be moved. Neither can Ormond, Dean or Hacht!'

'I know it carries risk—'

'It carries more than *risk*!'

Lt Sjorgen sighed. 'But they will be moved and there's nothing you or I can do about it.'

'We'll see about that!'

Lt Sjorgen stopped him as he heaved himself forcefully to his feet. 'Dr Banducci, there's an open breakdown of the ceasefire and the camp is being dismantled. This is a tactical decision based on everyone's safety, and you of all people know that the welfare of the many outweighs that of the few.'

Sherazad could see Lorenzo grappling with his temper, his body rigid, his jaw muscles working. He must be feeling like she'd felt when she'd been denied the chance to extend her resuscitation efforts. Desperate, enraged—impotent!

He finally gained enough control and shot the curt question, 'You have intelligence there'll be an attack?'

'After yesterday's attack, the third in a week, all personnel are being relocated deeper into so-called neutral territory, while troops are mobilising to search out hostile parties. A definite pattern has emerged, targeting humanitarian and peace-keeping efforts with an eye for maximum losses, probably to force us all out of the region so the war continues.'

Lorenzo absorbed the information, his scowl fixed on the drab olive canvas wall. He must have connected it to the attack on Sherazad's convoy for he asked in alarm, 'Have there been any more attacks on GAO operations or personnel?'

'Not that we know of, no. And they're being assigned more military protection as we speak.'

Lorenzo was silent for a moment, then he asked, 'So, you want us to go with our patients wherever you decide to dump them?'

The younger man's tired blue eyes closed, as if he too was trying to curb his temper. Then he opened them and bore head on Lorenzo's intimidating golden blaze. 'I know how you view those of us who chose to pursue a medical career in the armed forces—'

'You know *nothing*, Lieutenant Sjorgen!' Lorenzo cut him off, his voice an ominous bass rumble she'd never heard before.

The man was undaunted by Lorenzo's cold fury. 'I may know more than you think.' Sherazad wondered what that meant, and why it brought that violent gleam to Lorenzo's eyes. 'As hard as it is for you to believe, we're doctors too, bound by the same oaths you're bound by, or I would have transferred your patients behind your backs and assigned any other capable surgeon or critical care doctor to them. But continuity of care is vital to them. Only you know their case particulars, and that will mean the difference between their lives or deaths.'

'I can re-operate on Sergeant McFadden in twenty-four hours,' Lorenzo said. 'But it'll be at least a week before I sanction moving him. Or any of the others.'

Lt Sjorgen shook his head in regret. 'They're being moved today. You know in a tactical evacuation the injured are always transferred first.'

'Then you may as well kill them now.'

'Dr Banducci, please! They're stable now and with you along we have every hope they'll remain so until you reach the next aid station.'

'Are these Colonel LaCroix's orders?'

'Yes, but—'

Lorenzo didn't wait to hear the rest, but stormed out of the tent. With an uncertain look of apology to Lt Sjorgen, Sherazad ran after him.

For the next two hours she kept doing so as she was introduced to yet another Lorenzo: a hellraiser.

He contacted his headquarters, then every other military and peace-keeping installation in the region, demanding and getting their commanders, and giving them a large piece of his mind. In the end, he managed to obtain permission to stay at the camp with his patients for as long as he deemed it necessary for them to survive a transfer. He had permission to have all the personnel who agreed to stay, and to get his own personnel over, while the commanders would try to guard against any attacks. No promises, of course.

Colonel LaCroix was not happy with those amendments to his orders.

She and Lorenzo were heading to check on their critical patients when he intercepted them, a thunderous expression on his face.

'Dr Banducci.' His metallic voice clanged in anger. 'I've revised my opinion that your arrival was a stroke of luck. You may have done a lot of good, but now you're a hazard. You care only about your charges but so do I about mine! I'm not leaving any of them here to be blown apart in another terrorist attack like those soldiers we received yesterday. You want to stay, stay alone.'

'He won't stay alone, Colonel.'

That was the first thing Sherazad had said in two hours. It stopped Colonel LaCroix's tirade. And Lorenzo's heart.

He'd thought it went without saying she'd leave, go where it was safe. Relatively so, anyway. He'd arranged for his personal assistants in the Badovnan operation to fly over to form the medical team his patients needed.

'No, I won't, Sherazad, but it won't be you who'll keep me company. You're going to GAO headquarters.'

She shook her head. 'They're my patients too. In fact, Hacht and Ormond are more my patients than yours.'

'Listen—'

'I'll leave you to indulge in more ridiculous posturing, then,' the colonel growled. 'I have 325 personnel to evacuate and 3700 troops to mobilise. *Adieu*, Dr Dawson, Dr Banducci.'

He walked away without another glance. They didn't spare him one either. Lorenzo had eyes only for the little virago staring up at him, daring him to contradict her.

'You're not staying here, Sherazad, and that's final!'

'Why?'

Her single-word question threw him. It was the most logical one to ask, the only one to be expected really, but it still stymied him. His reasons were all primal and male and intensely unreasoning. He couldn't even begin to explain them, let alone defend them. Not even to himself. He had one way out of this.

'Because I said so.'

She gave him a mocking flutter of her lashes. 'Charmed, Dr He-Man! But what changed your mind? You were preaching brutal triage and sacrificing the unsalvageable. Now you're endangering yourself, a perfectly salvageable and useful life, to save patients who may not survive no matter what you do.'

'It's my life I'm endangering, not someone else's...' His

forceful argument stuck in his throat when he realised the trap she'd laid for him. She snapped it shut.

'But you *are* willing to endanger your other co-workers' lives, who know and accept the stakes, as I do. So why not *me*?'

Finding no way out at the moment, he resorted to ignoring her. 'I have no time for this. I have to see my patients.' He turned to head towards Critical Care.

She fell in step with him. '*Our* patients.'

He didn't answer. He wouldn't enter into a circular argument with her. She was going, and that was that.

Inside, they were met by François and the two critical care nurses. They immediately handed Lorenzo the patients' charts and answered his rapid-fire questions.

'McFadden's gas embolism has resolved and his hypothermia responded only to intravenous warm fluids, as you predicted,' François reported. 'But we needed a lot of those to bring his blood pressure to an acceptable level, though urine output is still unsatisfactory.'

Sherazad knew that the inflammatory reaction to the massive trauma caused extensive tissue and bowel swelling. Most of the fluids pumped back into McFadden were pooling there and not entering his circulation—hence his low blood volume and pressure, and reduced urine output.

'Give him dobutamine,' she said absently, as she pored over the charts Lorenzo had handed her, trying not to wince at the sight of McFadden's plastic-covered abdominal contents. 'It will open up blood capillaries and help fluid return from swollen tissues, taking down the swelling and increasing urine excretion. Also place a right cardiac catheter. We need to monitor his cardiac output and the efficiency of oxygen delivery.'

Both men turned their heads to her in surprise, and she bristled. Damn them both, anyway! Why should they be surprised? She was a qualified A and E doctor, wasn't she?

Lorenzo reverted to his ultra-efficient self in a second, conducting a comprehensive examination of his patient. 'Dr

Dawson's suggestions are excellent,' he said. 'And before you disappear on us, I want the lab to give me a few more readings…' He recited the tests he wanted repeated, and François jotted them down. 'And I'm not satisfied with his bleeding/clotting time. Give him another six units of fresh frozen plasma, plus two units each of cryoprecipitate and platelets.'

François nodded as he wrote down Lorenzo's treatments and handed him Delinski's chest X-rays. After glancing at them Lorenzo passed them to Sherazad.

'Rib fractures, wire-closed sternum, a missing lung lobe, but everything else looks almost normal!' She was astounded. That was the man who'd had his heart punctured and his chest blasted then sawn open. The man she'd given up on as dead twenty-four hours ago!

'His four chest tubes yielded very little blood too.' Lorenzo sounded engrossed as he examined his patient.

'What—what procedures did you do on him?' There— she'd asked. She could finally bear looking at the man she felt she'd chosen over another human being to save.

Lorenzo's gaze rested on her. She could swear he was reading her mind. His eyes softened, darkened to whisky, and he seemed about to say something. Then he clearly changed his mind and exhaled. 'I initially removed the detached parts of his left lung, and ligated many bleeding vessels. But the anaesthetist reported persistent tracheobronchial bleeding, so I had to resect a whole lobe. His cardiac injury was thankfully small and the bolstered mattress sutures I'd inserted in Emergency were enough. The worst part was a wounded coronary artery. With no chance of a cardiopulmonary bypass here, I had no alternative but to tie it and hope for the best.'

'He's still in better condition than McFadden,' she whispered.

Lorenzo gave her an understanding nod as he jotted down instructions for Delinski's continuing care. 'Although chest injuries are more rapidly fatal in the acute stage than abdominal ones, they're more easily treated with one definitive operation. But having presented from the field with an open injury, Delinski's infection risk is infinitely higher, even with the massive antibiotics cover. And with that tied coronary he may develop anything from angina to infarction.'

Later, they performed a meticulous re-evaluation of the rest of the patients before walking out of Critical Care.

Sherazad turned to Lorenzo the second they were alone, a finger tracing his shoulder, a teasing smile dancing on her lips. 'It's about time I sutured your wound. Or should I say *my* wound?'

Lorenzo's every muscle clenched at her light touch. The beauty of her and of her smile had something hot and fierce flooding inside him.

'And afterwards you'll go where you were originally headed.' In fact, he wanted to send her as far away as would ensure her safety. Back home even. Wherever her home was. He frowned. Could he possibly feel this much for someone he knew next to nothing about? Not that it mattered at the moment—what he didn't know, what he felt, or why! He had a job to do. She had to be safe. 'I'll catch up with you later.'

'I'm here to do a job, Lorenzo. And I'm going to do it.'

'I'm your boss and I'm saying you'll do it somewhere else.'

'Well, *I'm* saying save your breath and orders, *boss*.'

Her saucy but adamant resolve started a slow burn of anger in his gut. It twisted there with the overwhelming urge to drag her back to their tent and continue what Sjorgen had interrupted. He forced himself to focus. 'Sherazad—'

She cut him off again. 'I'm staying with you, Lorenzo.'

CHAPTER SIX

'SCALPEL, Gulnar! And I would appreciate some *real* suction too.'

Lorenzo's nurse jumped at his brusque order, crooning a breathless, 'Yes, Lorenzo!'

A sick feeling invaded Sherazad's bones as she watched the woman's obvious reactions, the hunger in her beautiful green eyes. She was gobbling Lorenzo up! Not that Lorenzo reciprocated. He only had glares to spare at the moment. But what about later?

Was this how it was between him and his nurse? Would she have to watch him picking up where he left off with Gulnar? Was this why he'd shut her out? In expectation of his lover's return?

She returned her attention to the operation with a supreme effort, focusing on his gifted hands as he carefully, but breathtakingly quickly cut out the dead tissue in McFadden's intestines and performed a meticulous end-to-end anastomosis, a reconnection of the intestines' ends.

He wrapped up the procedure in continuous growls for more instruments, and more cooing compliance from Gulnar. Sherazad tried to tune out the woman's fawning, wondering if Lorenzo's almost frightening voice had ever been the velvet baritone that had caressed her senses every time he opened his lips.

It was forty-eight hours since they'd had their almost-clash, and he'd been like a tiger with thorns in his paws ever since.

At first Sherazad thought he was being protective, and while it infuriated her, it delighted her in equal measure. But then it started to look like he was just angry she'd refused to obey his orders. Or, worse still, that as soon as he knew he'd have his core team, his lover maybe, he had no more use for her.

The more she thought about it, the more it made sense. And the more the idea took root, the more it hurt. As nothing ever had.

'I asked you to remove the packs *around* the liver, not the liver itself!' Lorenzo barked at his first assistant, Derek Morgna.

Derek froze, casting him a puzzled look. 'What's got into you, Lorenzo? We're lucky we still have our heads attached the way you've been biting them off. We know you must be traumatised and—'

'And how about you do your job instead of marvelling at the sound of your own eloquence, Derek?' The golden glare that impaled Derek had them all cringing. 'You do remember that a haemostatic pack applied to the liver can stick to its tissues, that its removal can cause more bleeding? You *do* remember what to do before attempting its removal?'

'I was about to soak it in saline—'

'When? After you've yanked off the left lobe?' Lorenzo growled as he shoved Derek's hands away and performed the delicate task himself, removing the packs from around the fragile tissues of the injured liver and spleen.

By now Sherazad was worried. She'd seen Lorenzo in the worst situations possible and he'd never even come close to being so...volatile!

She didn't have long to ponder his reactions, for it was her turn to be on the receiving end of his scalding tongue.

'You *will* rotate the bowels for me some time *today*, won't you Sherazad?' His voice dripped sarcasm.

Suddenly it was too much. The way he'd ignored her for the last two days, moving out of their tent without even telling her. The way it had been driven home to her that she came at the end of a long line of panting females. And now! It no longer mattered what was eating him. She gave back as good as she got. '*If* you'd bothered to tell us what this operation entailed, what exactly you wanted us to do, *before* you started, we might have been more capable of complying with your temperamental, fault-finding demands.'

The anaesthetist, Ben Murdock, snorted a short laugh, Gulnar made an incredulous sound, and Sherazad felt the other two men, Derek and Emilio, sucking in their breaths and holding them, probably waiting for Lorenzo to blast her off the face of the earth. The way his eyes ignited, the way his nostrils flared beneath his mask, she expected him to. Then he closed his eyes and inhaled a long, ragged breath. When he opened them, they again transmitted the Lorenzo she'd come to know and love.

Love? No, *not* love. She couldn't even *think* that! No, *no*...

Thankfully, his careless answer cut short the frantic moment of self-confrontation. 'I didn't think I needed to explain.'

She bristled. Not only was he glossing over his harshness, he wasn't even conceding its unfairness.

He went on. 'But I should have anyway.' Big of him! '*Va bene, amici.* This is the second stage of the damage control surgery I performed on Sgt McFadden—the re-operation. The principles are five-fold. Removal of clots and abdominal packs, haemostasis—assuring no more bleeding sources, restoration of intestinal continuity, complete inspection of the abdomen to detect missed injuries, and finally abdominal wound closure.'

He directed his now neutral gaze at her. 'Having already taken care of steps one, two and three, we come to step four—inspection. This is where rotating the bowels comes in. This is what I want you to do...' He showed her how to rotate the bowels to the left and to the right. 'This is called medial visceral rotation, and it's to check if all collections of blood have been removed, and if there are no deeper injuries that we've missed.'

They put his explanations into practice, and he finally

sighed in satisfaction. 'No more injuries, thank God. His pulmonary contusion is also resolving. Sherazad, wash out the abdomen with saline. Gulnar, swab and suction. Derek, close the abdomen with standard mass closure to the sheath and routine skin closure. Emilio, hand Derek instruments and the largest two drains.'

Sherazad felt his eyes following their every move as they carried out his orders. With the last stitch she cut for Derek, Lorenzo said, 'Bring him out, Ben. Finish up, everyone, then bring him to Critical Care.' Then he stepped away from the table, dragged down his mask and stretched.

Sherazad bit her lip beneath her mask. It wasn't fair. She was angry with him. His leisurely feline motions shouldn't have awareness kicking in her gut. Gulnar made a curious sighing sound and Sherazad snatched a look at her. She only hoped her own reaction wasn't that explicit!

Lorenzo was striding out when he paused at the door and tossed over his shoulder, 'Great job, everyone.'

A moment of absolute silence followed his departure. Then everyone burst out talking at once, bombarding her with questions.

Sherazad's eyes darted between her four new teammates. She hadn't seen them outside the obscuring surgical garments yet. They'd arrived just as Lorenzo had started the operation and had replaced the camp's medical staff as his assistants. In answer to their questions, she held up her hands. 'Whatever you want to ask will have to wait till later. I have to check on our other patients.'

Their disappointed voices rose in unison, but she escaped with an apologetic shake of her head, shedding her overgarments and going through to Critical Care. Lorenzo was there.

She nodded to the remaining nurse, who was waiting for one of their team to replace him so he could join his departing colleagues, then joined Lorenzo by Delinski's side.

He spoke without even looking at her. 'They're almost all gone. François wanted to stay, and if he'd had a chance

Sjorgen would have, but they had their orders. They're leaving us enough provisions to last two weeks.'

Sherazad knew that. She'd watched in amazement as the camp was dismantled, leaving them quarters, kitchen-dining area and generators to sustain the six of them who were staying behind. And enough medical accommodation for their five charges.

'Are you sure we can't evacuate any of them?' She cast a look around at their patients, her voice a mere whisper even though they were deeply sedated.

'You can still go with them, Sherazad.'

She didn't care that he sounded drained, almost sad. Not when it seemed he couldn't wait to get rid of her. She didn't care either when her voice trembled. 'That wasn't what I asked. Will you give me a straight, surgically sound answer, please?'

Lorenzo inhaled a sharp breath. Sherazad couldn't help watching his chest expand, his sensually sculpted lips tighten in aggravation. Couldn't help her body's automatic response.

'Who would *you* evacuate?'

His irritated counter-question jogged her back to her concern for their patients. She knew she wouldn't move Hacht who'd just had a craniotomy, opening his skull to evacuate the blood that had collected in a subdural haematoma. And she had diagnosed Ormond with a far more severe pulmonary contusion than McFadden's. Moving either before they'd stabilised would be fatal. McFadden and Delinski were Lorenzo's cases, so he knew best. She wasn't sure, though, about Dean.

At her silence, he exhaled heavily. 'I know risks of mobilisation seldom come up in civilian surgical practice. You probably never came across it, since you're not a surgeon. I also realise you think Dean is OK…' Now, *how* did he know what she was thinking? 'But he needs at least two weeks after the extensive grafting that repaired his femoral and popliteal arteries' injuries. His wounds are still open to avoid the high infection risk after his messy field injury. Evacuation, by air or land, would cause his grafts to come undone. He'd die of massive haemorrhage before they could do anything about it.

'As for McFadden, besides his own femoral artery repair, moving him before his complications are brought under control, before his bowels move and his wounds start to heal, would be as fatal as putting a gun to his head. If you're talking about him...' Lorenzo suddenly pulled her outside into the surgical holding area. 'I thought Delinski *might* withstand the transfer. At dawn, I tried a small experiment— a transfer to another bed. He went into ventricular fibrillation the moment he was moved. His heart resumed only after the third shock.'

She winced. If such a small move made Delinski's heart's rhythm go haywire, then the tied coronary artery had really compromised his heart's blood supply. Until collateral circulation kicked in, moving him was out of the question.

Lorenzo went on, intent, compelling. 'But they're only five patients, and we're capable of achieving and maintaining their stabilisation. You can go...' His hands came up to her shoulders, and she nearly cried out with the feelings the simple contact evoked in her. She jerked backwards, and he let his arms drop to his sides.

She couldn't bear it any more. She had to know.

'Will you, please, give me a straight answer? Why do you want me to leave so badly? Am I so incompetent? So...replaceable? Or are you just embarrassed about those kisses we shared, and you want me out of your sight so you won't be reminded of them? Are you regretting the way you've conducted our relationship so far, and now you want to put me firmly in my place as your subordinate? If you're afraid I'll pursue you or something then you're—'

'A fool!' he growled, closing the gap between them and hauling her into his arms. 'That's what you are. *How* did you reach all those ridiculous multiple-choice conclusions?'

She pushed herself out of his arms. She had to, or else

collapse at his feet in a puddle of longing. 'They're not so ridiculous. They're quite logical, given your behaviour in the last two days.'

'And you couldn't even guess the real and only reason for it?' He reached out to her again, this time only caressing her hair, her face.

Her heart lurched even at this light touch, making her gasp the question.

'And that is?'

'I want you safe.' He said it so simply that the very simplicity drove his sincerity into her heart.

He meant it.

Now she knew he did, she gave in to her longing. She turned her lips into his caressing palm.

'Then who's being ridiculous?' His hand convulsively pressed to her lips, as if to catch her murmured words, deepening the contact before slipping to weave into her hair, to cup her head. She surrendered to his hungry gesture, tipping her head back in his grasp. 'We're in the middle of a war, so nowhere's safe. Who's to say they won't be attacked as they retreat? That their relocation site won't suddenly become the next target? What if, by leaving, they've made this the safest place to be at the moment?'

He blinked his surprise. '*Dio, piccola!* Those possibilities never even crossed my mind.'

'So, since danger is everywhere, I'd rather be in danger with you.' At her whispered words, her name formed silently on his lips. She wet hers, where she could swear his taste lingered—for all time, it seemed. He followed her tongue's movements, something wild coming into his eyes.

His hand tightened in her hair, bunching a thick tress and tugging, before knotting into a trembling grip. Pleasure spikes shot from her every hair root to her toes. She leaned into him, feeling the sensual whirlpool he generated tugging her under. His other hand swept her curves, up her hip and waist to cup her breast. 'You shouldn't say things like that…' His thumb found and stroked her nipple. '*Do* things like that, *innamorata*, or I—'

The next second, his team members burst in on them *en masse*. They only had time to extricate their hands from around each other, leaving her swaying with the loss of his touch and the frustration of his unfinished ultimatum.

'They almost removed everything from *underneath* us.' The complainer was Derek, whom she now saw as a lanky, ash-blond man in his late twenties.

'That's what evacuation means, *amigo*,' Emilio Fernandez, Lorenzo's other nurse, a huge, dark and distinguished-looking man of Lorenzo's age, said matter-of-factly. 'Scheduled and thorough. Not like someone I know!'

Derek ignored Emilio's taunt, clearly as aggravated by military medical protocol as Lorenzo. 'But what will we do if we need to reoperate? What good is a stripped theatre?'

Lorenzo placated him. 'They know we have our own instruments. We'll manage. Now I must go over the details of *our* evacuation when it's time, and emergency measures in case anything goes wrong.'

With one last intense look into Sherazad's eyes, he turned and strode away.

'Want some company?' That was the openly eager Gulnar who, distressingly, turned out to be a glorious redhead. She was a few years older than Sherazad's thirty years, but she'd still be gorgeous at sixty. Lorenzo waved away her offer without turning and continued on his way.

They all pounced on Sherazad the second he was out of earshot.

'Sherazad Dawson, isn't it?' Ben, a balding, intensely blue-eyed handsome Englishman in his early forties, shook her hand with a lazy smile.

'You were with the convoy heading for the Sredna refugee camp?' Gulnar asked. 'The one that was attacked?'

She nodded and Derek said, 'We were supposed to join you. And we thought we'd never find Lorenzo. We certainly never expected to join you and find him *this* way…'

Emilio interrupted him. 'I can't tell you how horrified we were about your team members. We're still praying more survived.'

'It's an outrage, attacking humanitarian operatives.' That was Derek again, his heightening colour indicating how passionately he felt about the whole thing. 'All the reports about the attack were vague. Even Lorenzo didn't give us a clear picture about what happened, or how he came to be on the scene.'

'Or how you managed to make it here!' Emilio added.

'*And* he said nothing about his kidnapping,' Derek piped up again. 'So what happened to him? We thought he was shot in the ambush! But was it his kidnappers? Did they torture him or something? Was that what turned him into such an intolerant brute?'

Ben grinned. 'Lorenzo is an exacting taskmaster, terrifying even at ease. But seeing him in a temper was... something. Though nothing like the way you defused him.'

'You sure know how to tame the savage beast, Dr Dawson.' Emilio chuckled, his dark eyes gleaming in appreciation.

Gulnar laughed too. 'And I'm curious how you managed it. When he barked at me I nearly forgot what a scalpel was!'

'Only when he barked?' Emilio's derisive words were light, but his eyes were anything but.

Sherazad suddenly realised there were intense undercurrents between him and Gulnar. Was Gulnar involved with both men? But no—she somehow knew Lorenzo would never poach on another man's ground. So maybe Gulnar was Lorenzo's former lover, still—understandably—interested, Emilio was the new lover, jealous...

And maybe she was totally wrong. She really hoped she was...

For heaven's sake! Why should she care about Lorenzo's former lovers?

Because you think of yourself as his current one, that aggravatingly truthful voice inside her said, sniggering.

Well, she wasn't, she answered it forcefully.

Yet, it concluded the debate.

She would have argued further, but she had to answer her new team members' hail of questions. Or avoid them. She had no answer to some, and no wish to answer the others.

'The attack was so sudden, so vicious. I remember thinking I was going to die, then there was Lorenzo, saving me and driving the truck away. Then we drove here since he knew the way. As for his kidnapping or anything else, you'll have to ask him. I haven't a clue.'

Ben whistled. 'Sure you're not a secret agent, Dr Dawson? You realise you've told us less than nothing, don't you?'

'And it seems we'll have to be satisfied with that.' Emilio guffawed in agreement.

Those two took her reticence in their stride and went to tend to their patients. Derek and Gulnar persisted in asking prying but admittedly good-natured questions about her and Lorenzo's ordeal and relationship. Sherazad gave them non-committal answers until even they gave up.

Finally making good her escape, she went in search of Lorenzo.

Outside, the majestic but harsh Balkan landscape once again filled her with a sense of insignificance. The daunting mountains all around the purposely isolated camp seemed to have moved closer, closing in on them now that most of the camp had gone. A sudden kick of fear slowed her steps and blood roared in her ears, drowning out the receding thunder of the trucks carrying the camp and its personnel away. The military troops had already deployed twenty-four hours ago.

They were really going to stay here alone.

This certainly wasn't in GAO's brochure detailing the different possibilities and hazard levels of a frontline medical experience. But, then, what else that had happened in the last week was?

There should have been more warnings. Most of all, about her new boss. But Lorenzo didn't need a warning attached to him. His hazard was all too obvious. Even if she'd met him in the mildest, safest circumstances, he would have turned her world upside down anyway.

CHAPTER SEVEN

'SO—WOULD you like your daily dose of humble apologies now, or with dessert?'

Sherazad gazed into Lorenzo's incredible eyes across the table and nearly drowned. A jolt of delight buzzed up her spine and her heart performed a few physical impossibilities in her chest. She stuck out her tongue at him and he only laughed out loud, rich and deep and reason-annihilating.

Twelve days had passed. No one had come near their camp and their patients were finally doing well—as well as they'd hoped, anyway. And Lorenzo had turned his bout of boorishness into a running joke.

It was Derek who gloatingly answered him. 'I'll take mine now, thank you.'

'Careful, kid!' Lorenzo turned on him, mock-snarling. '*You* I don't owe any apology to, liver-yanking lad.'

'Hey...' Derek started to object but the rest, all present for a meal for the first time, burst out laughing, emotional and physical exhaustion tingeing their humour with hysteria.

Lorenzo had told her they could handle five critical patients without her, but even with her, the workload had kept them flat out for most of their waking hours. But she'd discovered they were a great team, smooth and practised, and very easy to get along with. She even got to like Gulnar who, apart from the fatal flaw of lusting after Lorenzo, was a superior nurse and a sweet woman.

Lorenzo was an awesome team leader. He kept them on their toes, kept their spirits up, prevented any friction and got round any mistakes. Not that there were any significant instances of either.

'At least I recognised Hacht's deterioration!' Derek mumbled as their laughter eased.

'That you did.' Lorenzo patted him on the back. He kept the jokes up, but he made sure each one of them felt valued. 'It took some sharp critical care skills to recognise his impending malignant brain swelling early enough for us to do something about it. And remind me to kneel at Daniel Plummer's feet for dragging me to assist him as many times as he did. Otherwise I wouldn't have dared reopen the craniotomy. But I'll be ecstatic when I can leave neurosurgery to him—when *any* specialist takes Hacht off my hands. Not that all of you weren't amazing help. Especially you, Ben.'

Ben raised his coffee-cup in weary salute. 'A closet neurosurgeon, that's me.'

'And thank heaven Sherazad's a closet respiratory therapist,' Emilio sighed, slouching flaccidly in his chair.

The aftermath of Hacht's crisis had left them all in a stupor. Each of their patients had suffered complications, ended with Ormond's full-blown adult respiratory distress syndrome and subsequent multi-organ failure. Sherazad had had the most experience with the grave and possibly fatal complication, and she almost ate and slept by his side for the five days it took him to pull through.

They exchanged more purposely bright conversation until they finished their meal. Then as they pushed themselves to their feet, each heading to his or her chores or off-duty time, Gulnar stopped Lorenzo with a clingy hand on his arm. 'Did you arrange for us to leave tomorrow, Lorenzo, or are you keeping us here longer?'

Sherazad couldn't help watching Lorenzo as he turned to his nurse, constantly looking for signs of attraction on his side. She was endlessly relieved that she saw none. The vibes directed towards Gulnar were all emanating from Emilio. But the Azerbaijani beauty was either totally oblivious of, or totally uninterested in, the Portuguese man's attraction to her.

'We're leaving.' Lorenzo answered Gulnar with all the

neutral ease he showed his male team members, moving out of her reach. 'Reports of the Sredna refugee camp are appalling, and it's time we did something about it. Our five boys here are going to survive the transfer now.'

Minutes later he followed Sherazad into their tent. He'd moved back in with her the day the camp had been evacuated. She hadn't commented. Neither had any of the others. Surprisingly, not even Gulnar.

Not that there was anything to comment on. She and Lorenzo were rarely together in the tent, and when they were, one of them was usually fast asleep. When she was awake and watching him sleeping, it was agony. But, then, so was every moment of every day, just being near him or constantly thinking of him. Not to mention being exposed to his hunger for her. He didn't try to hide it, yet didn't act on it, just being his wonderful, teasing self again. It was driving her to distraction.

His heavy-lidded gaze on her now made her sink onto her bunk, setting off a chain reaction of yearning inside her. But his eyes contained something besides desire, something they had contained a lot of lately. Questions. The questions she dreaded.

It seemed he had decided now was the time to ask them. 'Why are you here, *piccola*?'

Her heart thumped. Trust him to ask the one question that only the whole truth would answer. To escape it, she gave him her best cheeky smile. 'How many times will I tell you why I stayed?' He answered her evasion with an indulgent grimace, and she attempted a chuckle. 'Is it important why I'm here?'

'To me, yes.' He smiled back at her, that gorgeous smile of his that made everything right with the world. She couldn't believe how her wellbeing had come to rely on his approval, her security on his presence. How she'd almost shrivelled up when he'd deprived her of both, if only for a short time.

'If you'd rather not tell me…'

She rose from her bunk. She needed to take her eyes off him and her mind off images of them entwined there. 'If you think your reverse psychology will have me falling over myself, saying, "No, no, of course I'll tell you!" think again.'

He shrugged easily, his smile broadening. 'It usually works. But on normal people, not on Sherazads!'

Normal. The word slammed into her, smearing her vision in red. Deep, angry, violent red.

'And what do you mean by *that*?'

Lorenzo blinked in surprise at her sudden aggression. 'By what?'

'You think I'm not "normal"? Is that why you're asking why I'm here? Is that the real reason you were so eager to ship me off? Afraid I'm a ticking bomb or something?'

Lorenzo's mouth dropped open at her tirade. And stayed open. Where had *that* come from?

He shook his head, cleared his throat. 'It's OK, you're under too much pressure—'

'Don't you patronise me!' This time she nearly shouted, her voice having a sharp edge of fury that made him wince. 'What gives you the right to throw comments like that around? What's so *ab*normal about me?'

'*Dio, piccola!* I was only joking and, believe it or not, complimenting you. I do think you're unusual, in the best sense possible.' He smiled again, trying to coax her, to turn things back to the teasing level. 'I did think something was wrong when I spoke to you in every language under the sun and you just stared dumbly at me...'

'Yes, well, *you* were too dumb to try English first!'

Her vehemence dealt him a sobering blow. This was serious. But why? Only one thing came to mind. 'Are you still angry with me for being such a pig to you all those days ago?'

'So you realise what you were, you—you...!' Her words were choked, her eyes full, her colour a dangerous crimson. 'Did you do it on purpose so I would leave? And I don't care if you had the best motive in the world! Did you think I was so stupid, so immature, so unprofessional I'd leave my patients in a temper tantrum because my boss wasn't being nice to me any more?'

Lorenzo stared at her. *This* was the woman who'd weathered the worst crises with him? Who'd fought him and beside him with the ferocity of a tigress and the efficiency of a seasoned professional? About to break down on account of one stupid, harmless word?

It could be a reaction to the trials of the past weeks, an emotional outlet. But he couldn't bear the wild, accusing look in her eyes. He had to protect her from her anguish. He reached out to her. She fought him off with a violence that shook him.

'*Basta*, Sherazad, *basta*!' He tried to restrain her flailing arms gently, but she just shoved him and swung around to run away. He caught her back into a fierce hug, reverting to ragged Italian in his agitation. '*Sono spiacente, così spiacente! Non dovrei dire quello. Perdonilo. Chiedo scusa, mia tesoro.*'

'You should be sorry!' Her hiss shook as hard as she did. 'And, no, you shouldn't have said that and, no, I don't forgive you, and *stop* calling me your treasure!'

She'd understood every word he'd said! He hugged her harder, a wavering laugh escaping his tight throat. 'That odd word you know of Italian is certainly comprehensive!'

He turned her around, keeping her pressed in the circle of his arms. This time she didn't pull away, her eyes lifeless with an inner agony he'd never seen before. It hit him in the gut with enough force to make him breathless. He had to know what it was, had to ease it somehow. The urge stunned him. He didn't get close, never got involved in others' turmoil.

But this was Sherazad. And it was too late. He was already too close. Already involved.

He still tried to stop. He couldn't. He found himself urging her. 'Sherazad, tell me, please, why are you so defensive, so angry? Who hurt you? What are you running from?'

'I thought you were a surgeon, not a psychoanalyst, Lorenzo.' Her tone was caustic, but he could feel her wavering. His heart hammered in anticipation and dread. She was going to tell him why. Why she'd ventured to the frontline, why she'd been scared of his passion, why she'd exploded in anger at his inane joke. Somehow he knew it all tied in together.

He didn't want to find out, yet he couldn't wait to.

'I don't know why I flared up, especially since I know you joke about everything. I guess I'm just tired.'

He pressed her harder, although he knew she'd feel the effect she was having on him. She did.

'I can't even think when I'm feeling you this way!' Her protest took on a sultry tone that distracted him from his purpose, inflaming him even more. He hardened—no, better look for a less distressing word—he *stuck* to his resolve. He wasn't giving her excuses not to tell him the secrets eating away at her, the heartaches she needed to share.

He eased her away just enough for them not to be plastered together, but held onto her still.

Did he think that was better? Sherazad nearly scoffed out loud. She was melting from the inside out. Her legs had long become boneless, and her heart wouldn't let her hear her own voice.

But he was waiting to hear her pathetic story, and suddenly she wanted to tell him and get it over with.

She couldn't do it while she looked into his eyes. She closed hers and put her head on his chest. It moved beneath her cheek in a great breath. She managed a choked one, then started.

'I was at a place in my life where I was feeling so sorry for myself, and I hated it. I hated what had happened to me—what I *let* happen to me—and I was damned if I was going to wallow in self-recrimination and pity. The day I went to apply for a new job, I saw GAO's drive for doctors on the frontline. It was a wake-up call. A reminder of how much worse off other people are all over the world. I didn't know if I could be of any help, but I believed I'd at least be helping *me*, putting my own life in perspective. So, you see, I'm not benevolent at all.'

His amused but gentle laugh rumbled beneath her ear, tingling right down to her soul. 'I hate to disillusion you, but you're not unique. Most come to the frontline with less than purely humanitarian motives. Most are exorcising some sort of demon. But it doesn't matter why you came—what matters is that you did come, what you do while you're here. So my opinion of you not only holds, it's even better now.'

She shook her head, trying to contradict him, but he pressed her head harder to his chest, pressing a fierce kiss to her forehead. 'Yes, it is. Stop selling yourself short. But you've told me nothing, you evasive *bambola*.'

She snuggled her face in his warm chest, murmuring into it, 'Not evasive—not a doll.'

'Yes, you are. *My* evasive doll. So, are you escaping a dark past with some sort of secret agency?'

She had to chuckle, recalling Ben's and Emilio's similar assessment. But, raising her eyes to his empathetic ones, she finally knew she could share her humiliating secrets with someone. She who would have rather choked than tell anyone, starting with her family.

She laid her head on his heart again. 'My life was normal, as far as normal goes, until I met Jack…'

Jack. Lorenzo tensed in spite of himself. So there *was* a man at the heart of this.

'He was our hospital's newest consultant and he pursued me from the moment he saw me. I was very…flattered. He was divorced, but I didn't press for details. I didn't think it was any of my business, even when I accepted the occasional date. I didn't think in terms of anything serious. Certainly nothing intimate to start with, as my limited experience in that area had been…disappointing, and he seemed willing to let me set the pace.

'But soon I knew it would go nowhere. We had nothing in common. I tried to let him down easy, but he tried so hard to please me he made me feel guilty. For months. At last I told him, and he asked for one last date, a friendly goodbye. He seemed to accept my decision, but after drinks he rushed me to my apartment. I vaguely thought he was in a hurry to get rid of me, now he'd made certain I wouldn't change my mind. The next thing I remember was waking up in bed, naked...'

She moved out of his suddenly weakened arms, and this time he didn't have enough power or co-ordination to stop her, unbearable images filling his mind.

'He said, though I seemed drunk, I knew what I wanted, that I asked him in, asked for sex. He laughed, saying that maybe he should have offered me Martinis before. I do have a low threshold for alcohol and I did have two drinks, trying to harden my heart. As I remembered nothing, I had to take his word for it. Anyway, I told him I hadn't been aware of what I'd said or done, that it was still over. I felt so ashamed...'

'How *could* you be?' Lorenzo choked, his mind disintegrating with hatred for the man who'd taken advantage of her.

'I'm telling you how I felt, not that I was *right* to feel it.' She suddenly sagged on her bunk and started smoothing the covers with insistent, trembling strokes. 'I was mostly glad it was over. But it wasn't. I was pregnant.'

'*Dio!*'

'I went into a rage and told him. If I'd been drunk, *he* should have protected me. He said I took him by surprise, that he'd wanted me for so long he lost his head. After that, he was everywhere, demanding to get married, to give our baby the home it deserved. I didn't have any tempting experience with men or commitment, and I wasn't even thinking of getting married at that time, certainly not to him. Still, it seemed the best thing to do...'

No! He wanted to roar it, as if it would make a difference, make her change her mind in retrospect, rewrite history.

'It was the baby... I couldn't bear having an abortion. And my family... I couldn't bear disappointing them—their golden girl, turning up with an illegitimate child...

'So we married, and he charmed my family, the way he'd charmed me to begin with. He said we'd start over, have a *normal* marriage. I tried, but I couldn't...feel anything with him. In fact, I felt repulsed, then disgusted. He soon started to tell me what an abnormal woman I was, that it was no wonder two men before him had found me a frigid bitch. His accusations found their mark. He had a reputation as a Don Juan, and I already doubted my ability to enjoy sex. I certainly wasn't giving him what a man wants from his wife. So I excused him. But he got steadily rougher. After each failed time, he got more abusive, getting jealous, going into rages. He hit me a couple of times, then fell at my feet and begged my forgiveness, made a very convincing plea for himself, even made *me* feel guilty.

'I still excused him, until the time he told me it was better having sex with me unconscious. It was then that the doubts I had were solidified. I'm convinced he slipped a date-rape drug into my drink that first time—probably Rohypnol. It explained a lot, but I was still trapped. Married to him, carrying his baby, my family in raptures, thinking the world of him and already planning the baby shower. I still attempted to make the best of it, weak fool that I was...'

She raised her black eyes to him, and he almost fell to his knees before her, wanting to ask her forgiveness—for everything that had happened to her, for being helpless to change it. But there was more.

'He attacked my self-worth and confidence constantly—expertly—until I became so dejected, so unable to function I started making mistakes at work. He told me it was because I was incompetent and unbalanced and not to look for excuses. Heaven help me, I believed him more every day. Anyway, I feared I'd make irreparable errors, so I quit. At last he tried to—to sleep with me when I was eight months pregnant. I repulsed him and he…beat me up…'

She gulped a sobbing breath, and Lorenzo's heart almost burst out of his chest.

'I…lost the baby and I—I— Oh, God, I was *relieved*. I didn't want a child with this man, a child who'd have him as his father. I filed for divorce the same day, and my family, whom I'd kept in the dark, thought it was with shock over my stillbirth. They even tried to persuade me against it. For a year he fought me, lied about me, sued me even, and in between kept begging me for a second chance. In the end I got the divorce, but I still felt threatened…'

'You felt he might harm you?' Was that strangulated whisper his own?

'I didn't fear for my life, but certainly for my sanity.'

'So you ran away? You came here?'

'At first I did consider running away, but my backbone finally resurfaced. I refused to let him turn me into a fugitive. So I confronted him. For the first time he saw in my eyes my intention to really fight back. He may be obsessive and abusive, but his only strength was my weakness, as you once said. He backed off.'

Something lit up her eyes and his breath caught at the sight. 'So, this is my sorry, stupid story.' She was even smiling in self-deprecation. 'My family tried everything to stop me from coming here, but I was determined. Then I came and promptly fell into a *real* disaster. It certainly blasted things into perspective. Everything that had happened to me in the last two and a half years looked laughable in comparison.'

'I'm…glad you feel this…positive.' He felt his left arm going numb. Was he having a heart attack? He wouldn't be surprised.

His eyes clung to her every move as she rose to her feet fluidly and walked up to him, her eyes intent. 'Do you think the others need any help?'

He blinked at her unexpected question. 'No. Uh—why?'

'Because I think it's time you made love to me.'

CHAPTER EIGHT

'MAKE love to me, Lorenzo. No stopping this time.'

Sherazad heard the seductive words roll off her tongue on a husky, hungry purr, and nearly laughed out loud. In elation, for feeling so light and whole and *normal*, after she'd forgotten how that felt. In mischief, for having flabbergasted the imperturbable Lorenzo.

'Sherazad…'

She watched him struggle for something to say, and that laugh escaped at last. Happy and unfettered.

'I want you, Lorenzo. I've wanted you from the first moment I saw you.' She was amazed at her boldness. She'd really broken free. Thanks to him.

'You *shot* me the first moment you saw me!' He shook his head, still looking as if she'd electrocuted him.

She laughed again. 'No, I rammed the truck door on your head first, then tried to gouge out your eyes and bite mouthfuls out of you. And I never even apologised…' She reached out and caressed everywhere she'd hurt, her fingers eloquent with her impatient need. He shuddered. Then he shuddered harder and grabbed her hands. 'Let me make it all better…' She substituted her captive hands with her lips.

'It can't get any worse,' he groaned hoarsely, '*Pietà, tesoro…*'

She pressed herself against him, and felt the potency of his glorious arousal. Oh, my. She'd done *that* to him. Feminine power surged inside her. 'Don't beg, Lorenzo. It doesn't become you. And I'm pitiless right now…'

He still stood there, inert, until a niggling doubt made her snap her eyes up to his face. What she saw there…

Then it came. The most crushing humiliation of her life. The only one that reached her heart—and crumpled it.

How could she have not predicted his reaction to her pathetic story?

She'd disgusted him.

Mercifully, the outside world intruded, terminating the suffocating moment. An excited Derek called out outside the tent. 'Hey, guys, you still awake?' She jerked away, stumbling to let him in.

He bounced inside. 'They're sending in three military helicopters at noon tomorrow. Want us to start packing, Lor?'

Sherazad didn't wait to hear Lorenzo's reply, bolting out of the tent and walking blindly into the freezing, desolate night.

Lorenzo didn't know what he'd said to Derek. He was gone, so he must have answered his questions.

He wished Sherazad hadn't answered his.

He felt…sick. Sick with rage and regret.

He felt about to explode with futility and impotence.

Sherazad, his indomitable butterfly, in the grip of depravity, the prey of demoralisation and abuse. Wounded and scarred, probably for life. And he could do nothing about it.

It was unthinkable. Unbearable.

He fell to his bunk, his head falling into his hands.

Sherazad was wrong. What was going on around them wasn't that much worse than what she'd been through. At least in a war there were enough inhuman circumstances to explain human depravity—even if never to excuse or forgive it. But what could explain brutality when there was no motive but sheer perversion and cruelty?

His lungs closed, his muscles quivered.

His eyes burned.

He hadn't shed a tear since he was five. Except over Piero… He wasn't going to over Sherazad!

He heaved himself to his feet, wiping both hands over his face angrily. Sherazad was alive and well, and he was damned if he'd let anything happen to her again.

He winced as he made the adamant pledge to himself, another wave of sheer helplessness sweeping over him. For how could he ever keep it?

And how could he keep his hands off her now? And he'd thought moving back in with her had been torture before!

His earlier reservations about intimacy with her paled into insignificance. Now the stakes were infinitely higher. Making love to her would no longer only be the one thing he craved most in life, it would also be his life's most precarious responsibility.

For what if he disappointed her, too? Added to her self-doubts and bitterness, damaging her still more? Even if he didn't, what if she regretted it later? He had no illusions. She was on the rebound. She'd poured her heart out and probably felt liberated, however false the feeling might be, and was out to prove to herself she was no longer crippled by fears and inhibitions.

He *couldn't* greedily snatch at her the moment she offered herself. He had to give her time, and if afterwards, when she was thinking clearly, she still wanted him… What happened then?

This was impossible. He wanted her so much, he wanted to ignore everything, all considerations. And if it were only him who'd suffer, he would have. But he couldn't risk her well-being—his Sherazad…

He had to talk to her again. He didn't know what he'd say, or if he'd only make things worse, but he had to just be with her.

He put his thermal jacket back on and went in search of her.

In a minute he was rushing into the medical unit's interconnected tents, shivering and marvelling at the difference in temperature outside and inside. He'd almost frozen in the moments he'd been in the open air.

'What are you doing here?' Emilio frowned the moment he saw him. Then he turned his disapproval on Derek. 'I told you not to wake him. What can he do now?'

'He was awake,' Derek protested.

'And since you're here, sit down and I'll make you a cup of coffee.' Gulnar fluttered her lashes and perpetual invitation at him. He nearly groaned. What was wrong with the woman? He'd worked with her for five months before his kidnapping. How could she have not got his message yet? Or Emilio's?

'No, thanks, Gulnar,' he declined, escaping eye contact with both her and Emilio. 'Where's Sherazad?'

'Sher's sleeping.' That was Ben, walking in from Critical Care. 'Isn't she?'

Lorenzo paused for a second, suppressing the spurt of irritation Ben's easy familiarity with Sherazad always provoked in him. *Sher* indeed!

'She isn't. I thought she was here.'

Ben raised a magazine and looked underneath. 'No. She isn't *that* small.' He chuckled and Lorenzo had the ridiculous urge to blacken his blue eyes. Only the sudden fear rising inside him stopped him from making a biting reply.

'She's probably back in the tent now.' He exerted all his control to pretend to dismiss the subject, to ask for an update on their patients, then to walk out at a normal pace. He didn't want anyone suspecting anything was wrong, or following him out.

The second he was out, he gave in to his agitated feet's demands.

His sprint came to an abrupt halt a dozen feet later. The transition from the tent's lights to the cloud-obscured moon's had blinded him. He waited until his vision adjusted then shot forward again.

She was a rational woman, he kept telling himself. No matter how upset she felt, she wouldn't venture far from the camp. He'd find her in one of the other tents. But with each empty tent, his apprehension mushroomed until it became full-blown panic.

'*Sherazad!*'

His only answer was the dissipation of his frantic shout.

He opened his mouth to shout even louder when her distant 'What do you want?' detonated inside his head. He swung around and darted at full speed in the direction of her voice. He found her in the truck, the door open, one foot on the step. He exploded.

'Are you *crazy*?'

The word was out before he could stop it. He winced as he remembered her reaction to a far lesser word, and her reasons for it. But *he* was crazy, with fear, fury and relief.

'I must be.' Her chuckle was weak and bitter. 'To think Jack was right after all.'

'Shut *up*, Sherazad!' He surged up to scoop her in his arms. His left arm wasn't back to full power, but she was so small compared to him that he lifted her as if she weighed nothing. He had enough adrenaline coursing in his system he suspected he could have lifted the truck itself.

He ran with her to their tent, deposited her carefully on the bunk, darted to secure the door, then rushed to fill hot-water bottles.

She was shivering, thank God, so her core temperature was still within acceptable range. If he hadn't gone after her...

He shook off the horrifying possibilities, returned to her, tucking her beneath the covers, surrounding her with the bottles. She seemed dazed, but when he started taking off her freezing clothes, she resisted.

'You're hypothermic! Let me—'

She pushed his hands away in irritation. 'I'm not hypothermic! I was coming in when I saw you running around. I may be crazy, but I'm not stupid or suicidal!'

He glared at her when another shiver shook her. 'Mind telling me what you were doing out there in the first place?'

Her lips twisted. 'Haven't I told you enough for one night? Sure you want to hear more?'

There was more? He wasn't sure he'd survive hearing any more. But he had to know. 'Yes!'

'Why? Haven't I disgusted you enough already?'

'Disgust?' Incredulity froze the exclamation on his lips. Was that what she thought? Why she'd run? She thought his disgust was directed towards *her*? Furious concern unleashed his tongue. '*Dio!* Are you really crazy, or are you hallucinating with hypothermia after all?'

She hiccuped a distressed laugh. 'Maybe I should have stayed with Jack. We made one fine unstable couple.'

'Stop mentioning that *bastard's* name!' He stopped, raked his hands in his hair, then spoke again, trying not to shout this time. 'And how can I be disgusted? You were a *victim*...'

'What you feel doesn't have to be rational.' She suddenly closed her eyes, pain etched on her every feature. 'But it is natural. If *I* can be disgusted with myself—'

'Shut up, Sherazad, just shut up.' He crushed her in his arms, his heart stuttering. 'Think. You plastered your body to mine. You *felt* me. If you think that was disgust then you really know nothing about men.'

She struggled out of his arms so she could gaze at him, probing, wary. 'Your body could have reacted instinctively, independent of your mind. Male libido is famous for that.'

'You mean female libido isn't?' He attempted to smile through his pain and aggravation at her insecure logic. '*Tesoro*, arousal isn't always answerable to common sense, but it certainly is to disgust. Believe me, there's nothing more...deflating!'

She still looked so unsure, so vulnerable. 'Really?'

Every fierce and protective feeling in his soul rushed to crowd into his throat, blocking it. He just nodded.

She drew in a ragged sigh. 'It's ridiculous, isn't it? A thirty-year-old divorcee and would-be seductress who knows nothing about the ABC's of the male operating system.'

Laughter ripped out of him at her self-deprecating and unexpected words. He hugged her exuberantly, then withdrew to say, 'Lesson one in real men, *innamorata*—a real man does *not* get aroused by, or in spite of, ugly or violent emotions.'

She burrowed in his chest and nodded. 'If you say so.'

'I do.' He pressed her harder to him, her feel, her scent—everything about her—deluging his senses. 'Now to apply lesson number one—did any of the above apply to my condition then?'

She raised obsidian eyes to him. The dawning confidence there, and her soft hand's hesitant touch on his cheek sent his heart rocketing. Then she wriggled against him and it stopped. Her hand trailed down his body, singeing him even through his heavy clothes, down his chest, his clenched abdomen, then lower—and lower. His vision blurred. He hardened beyond agony. Then she made it worse, moaning, 'Not then—or now!'

He staggered to his feet, putting the breadth of the tent between them.

She heaved herself to a sitting position. 'What's this? Punishment for all the times I turned men down? I thought on-off manoeuvres were purely female.'

He nearly choked on his laugh. 'You keep saying the most ridiculous things! Off? What *harder* evidence do you need that you have me on almost all the time?'

'What good is evidence when it isn't backed by the proof of action, you incomprehensible man!'

'Lesson two in real men—being about to explode doesn't mean I can't hold back.'

'Who's asking you to?'

'Certainly not you.'

'*So?*'

So, indeed! He walked back to where she lay tangled in the covers, and sank to his knees beside her on the floor as if hypnotised. He was still tall enough to look down at her. To drown in the mystical eyes that filled his every thought, fuelled his every fantasy. To count the agitated rise and fall of breasts made for his pleasure, and to slip further into madness each time. She fidgeted, a whimper escaping her. She wanted this. Wanted *him*. The knowledge blazed through his body, with joy and savage desire.

He still couldn't give in. 'I still have no protection.'

'I do.'

He couldn't help letting his surprise show. He cursed himself for it when she scrambled to hide her face in his chest, her voice a shy, choked whisper. 'After Jack, I—I decided to…protect myself—just in case…'

Just in case she was raped again.

'Lorenzo!' Her hand clung to his, and he realised it had convulsed in her hair. He slammed a brake on his emotions and massaged her scalp, burying his trembling lips in her chameleon-gold tresses. He couldn't afford to let anything taint the tenderness he needed to lavish on her.

She was all that mattered now.

But he had to say a few things. Now he knew she was safe, it was almost impossible to say them. But they had to be said.

'Innamorata, what you feel, it could be the danger, our proximity, the physical deprivation—maybe a reaction to the ugly memories…'

'No!' Sherazad buried her hands in his hair, her voice a throb of silk and night and hunger. A groan of real agony escaped him. 'It's not a reaction to anything. I *want* you. I never knew wanting like this existed. I'd never regret it, if that's what you're afraid of. *Please*, Lorenzo…'

He knew then that the fight was over. But there was one more thing he had to say. One more thing he hated to say. 'Sherazad, *tesoro*—I've long accepted this…' he made an encompassing gesture '…as my vocation, my life. There's no place left in me for normality, for relationships.'

'Who needs either?' she cried out. 'Please, Lorenzo—I just need to know…'

He wanted to shout one last thing too. His greatest fear. *What if I disappoint you?*

But he swore to himself that he wouldn't.

Sherazad lay there, waiting for Lorenzo's reaction, quivering with anticipation. With too much hunger to bear. With dread.

She needed to know. But what if what she learned crippled her once and for all? What if, even wanting him more than she wanted anything in life, she was still unable to feel pleasure? Worse, what if she still proved to be the disappointment three men had already told her she was? She couldn't bear disappointing *him*…

But he was there, dissolving her fears in a kiss that left her in no doubt just how fiercely he wanted her too. She couldn't wait for him to tear her out of her clothes and show her just how fiercely.

Instead he stood up and slowly undressed, his tender gaze in direct contradiction to his wildness of seconds earlier. Suddenly, she understood. He was exposing himself first, putting himself at a disadvantage, showing her that, no matter how much he wanted her, he'd check himself. He'd already given her every evidence that her desires came first and foremost with him. Then her every rational thought evaporated…

Clothed, Lorenzo was in a class of his own. And she'd seen bits and pieces of him before. But seeing his full reality…

Her mouth actually watered as he dropped one garment after the other to the floor, and her hands stung with the need to touch, to marvel, to memorise his male power and grace.

'Oh, *Lorenzo*…' Was that her voice? That thick, covetous rasp? But who could blame her? He'd just stepped from her most outrageous fantasies. She'd never had a fantasy that extravagant. And he wanted *her*.

Still in those much-fantasised-about silk boxer shorts that did nothing to hide the fact, he moved back to her, in fluid motion, his muscles rippling and bulging as he knelt beside her again. Then he devoured her—with his eyes. She couldn't bear it. Tears stung her eyes and she almost wailed, 'Lorenzo! Don't make me beg any more…'

He swept her in his arms and pressed feverish kisses all over her face and throat, her mouth, groaning his answer deep inside her. 'Only if you let *me* beg *you*…'

She tried to wind herself around him, but he disentangled himself gently. 'Let me, *tesoro*…'

His hands trembled as he released her from clothes that had become suffocating. She tossed and whimpered. Her hands convulsed in his ebony hair, tugging at his silver wings. But he wouldn't hurry.

By the time he had her naked before him, she knew what erotic torment truly was. But it was all worth it, just to see his eyes—she cried out at the savage hunger in them. He closed them instantly, opened them again with it under control. Still afraid to scare her, the foolish man. When all she wanted was for him to let go of his control and just give her everything he'd got. At least he couldn't control the raggedness in his voice. '*Perfetta! Divina! Dio*, Sherazad—do you have any idea how beautiful you are?'

She thrashed her head on the pillow. '*You're* beautiful!'

He caught her head with gentle hands, pressed a fierce kiss to her lips. 'Then let me show you…how much I hunger for you—all of you…'

And he showed her. He drank her lips dry, then moved to her neck, her arms, her hands. She was quaking when he finally drew one of her fingers inside his hot mouth. The cramping between her legs clenched on another rush of molten agony. She hadn't known it could be like this. Then he sucked—hard.

She bucked off the bed. '*Lorenzo!*'

He was far from finished. He exposed her to all forms of sensual exploitation. He was everywhere. Kneading, kissing, licking. Nibbling, nipping and suckling. Her feet, down her back, all over her stomach. Her breasts, her buttocks, the insides of her arms and thighs. All the time coming up to plunge deep kisses into her mouth along with more aroused, arousing words. She lost count how many times she begged him.

'Don't rush me, *tesoro*—let me feast on you, worship you.' But he finally drew away and she thought he'd—at last—undress completely and join his body to hers. She rose to hurry him, welcome him…

The next second he swung her legs over his shoulders. She fell back in surprise. And consternation. She understood what he meant to do. She knew that women who couldn't climax through intercourse did that way.

But what if she couldn't even then?

It no longer mattered. Neither did the temptation of experiencing sexual release. All she wanted was intimacy with him, no matter the outcome.

She tried to sit up, panting, 'I want you, Lorenzo, *you*…'

'And you'll have me, every way you want me, but first…' He blew his hot, ragged breath on the knot of flesh where all her nerves converged. The sound that came from her was alien—hunger made audible. She was mindless now. Nothing remained in her but craving and sensation. The emptiness inside her was spreading, destroying her sanity, engulfing her.

'You're killing me—so empty, crumbling…'

In response he slipped a long, careful finger inside her.

She screamed. Her breathing and her heart stopped.

He soothed her back with a trembling but insistent hand, kneading her breasts, pinching her nipples, as the other drove deeper inside her. She thrashed and begged for him some more. He only added a second finger, then a third and quakes started, radiating from the point where her inner flesh clamped his fingers, rippling out violently, her every cell hurtling with frightening speed towards something she'd never imagined—something cataclysmic…

He rubbed his slightly scratchy face feverishly against her tender inner thighs, like a lion roughly nuzzling his mate, and when he growled he sounded like one. 'So hot and fragrant, so tight, so ready—dying to taste you…'

Then he did, and it was too much to bear. With his first voracious lick, she imploded, collapsing back on herself, becoming one tight pinpoint of insanity. She hovered there for one endless heartbeat. Then he sucked her flesh inside his mouth and she exploded. She ceased to exist, dissipated in wave after tidal wave of white-hot release.

In the beginning of a new life, the convulsions racking her body eased and she saw his regal head between her thighs, still suckling her, drawing out her aftermath, draining her of every spark of pleasure her body was capable of.

She closed her eyes and surrendered to his ministrations. Then her eyes snapped open. On stupefaction. Her pleasure was not subsiding, it was building, the screaming tension for release back in full force. He went on and on, until she was convulsing and heaving again, in the merciless grip of an even fiercer climax.

An eternity later, inside a body that was no longer hers to command and a mind that was no longer hers to access, she saw him rise, coming to her. Her focus sharpened on him, after it had been internalised.

And suddenly she felt like screaming.

She'd been duped. Ripped off. Cheated out of years of peace and fulfilment. There was nothing wrong with her.

Then she felt angry, at herself. Everything had been wrong with her own stupid choices.

And she felt like weeping. At his generosity, his selflessness, his restraint. At the enormity of what he'd given her.

She would have never believed that a man could deny himself this way when he'd been in an agony of arousal. When he still was.

But he just lay wrapped around her, caressing her in sweeping motions, murmuring praise and passion in that voice that spoke to her soul. 'Sherazad—beyond my fantasies…'

He was lulling her to sleep!

She didn't know what stunned her more. That he was doing that, or that he only managed to arouse her again. She wanted him even more now.

But this time she was taking no substitutes.

Lorenzo thought Sherazad was snuggling into him so she'd be more comfortable. Then he felt her warm, eager lips and hands on him and knew what she was after. He stopped her.

'You don't have to, *tesoro*.' He would have liked his voice to have come out steadier. This ragged whisper was all he managed. 'It's amazing enough knowing I've given you pleasure. Now sleep—you need your rest.'

She rose and gave him a smile that turned his arousal to steel and the rest of him to mush. 'I need *you*, so stop stalling!'

He closed his eyes against her overwhelming temptation. Until he heard her whisper, 'But if you don't need me…'

His eyes flew open to watch insecurity creeping back into her face. He was almost furious with her. 'Now, *that's* beyond ridiculous.'

'So what's the problem now?'

And he had to tell her. 'What if I disappoint you?'

She shook her head, her black eyes glittering with a new emotion, fierce and certain. 'You won't. You can't. Please, Lorenzo. I need you inside me…'

He met her fervent gaze, his will crumbling, his misgivings vanishing. 'And how I need to be inside you…'

He rose and, with a groan of mixed pain and relief, released himself. His groan was echoed by her gasp. He followed her gaze and was surprised himself. He'd never been this…engorged.

Coming back to her, he watched her expressive features shimmer with both desire and apprehension. He smoothed

her hair and parted her panting lips with a gentle, probing
kiss. Then he lay on his back.

'You take me, *tesoro*.'

Her eyes widened in shock and she shook her head. He
kept whispering encouragement to her, until she ventured
onto his lap. But after straddling him she stopped, her trembling hands stroking him in awe as he lay long and thick
against her belly. 'Take me inside you. Take your pleasure.
I'm yours.'

A wave of longing swept her face and she finally rose
and opened herself on him. He felt her molten tightness start
to engulf him, heard the mewling sound she made as he
began to stretch her. The pleasure was so acute he couldn't
stop his lusty shout. But he exerted everything he had so he
wouldn't thrust upwards to complete their union, his eyes
on hers assuring her that it was all on her terms.

Midway, she stopped, panting. 'I can't…take any
more…'

He stroked her buttocks, coaxing, soothing. 'Yes, you
can. You were made to fit me, to take me. Take your time,
enjoy me…'

Sherazad had stopped in anticipation of pain. Lesser men
had hurt her, or at best left her sore and frustrated. Surely
he was too big for her? Surely she'd start to hurt if she took
more of him? Not that she hurt at all now. She
felt…incredible. He felt incredible inside her. All her body
wanted was to impale itself on the rest of him. It somehow
knew it was created for that, for this man's body. Now his
hot words brought another rush of liquid madness flooding
her core. And she found herself sliding down, fulfilling its
craving.

She arched, her back a steep curve. Her mouth opened
on a soundless scream at the potency of the moment.
Pleasure detonated where he stretched her beyond her limits.
Then spread like wildfire to raze her body. He seemed to
fill her whole body. Fill her whole being.

She bucked, withdrew, so she could start all over again.

Pleasure, sharp and clawing, built. She reached eager hands to worship his features, luxuriating in his beauty. His hands reciprocated, roaming her as she rode him, every touch rich and tender, even in the inferno of passion.

He kept whispering driven words, now purely in Italian. But he held himself in check, letting her set the pace. Soon nothing was quick enough, or close enough. Her fingers twisted in his chest hair, dug into his steel muscles. His roar of pleasure liquefied her insides. She bent to brand his lips and his taste overloaded her senses. She broke the kiss only when they had to cry out in a frenzied duet. High and deep, with the sharp cresting waves of their mating.

She was desperate for him to remain inside her. Never to let it end. But she was desperate for release, unable to withstand the pleasure build-up. Unable to make another move. Why wasn't he *doing* something?

'Lorenzo!'

Mercifully, he understood her frenzied cry and took over. Supported her on his powerful legs and finally—finally— surged to her womb.

His thrust was the bolt of ecstasy she needed to topple over the edge. Her cries stifled, and his name squeezed out of her very depths as contractions imploded her, deluging her in the most intense release he'd given her yet.

She melted back against his support, all her pleasure centres saturated, holding his eyes with her satiated, grateful ones. But instead of joining her, he stilled, his face a watchful mask. Had he given her all that pleasure but didn't feel any himself? *No!*

But his whole body was taut, fine tremors of extreme tension breaking through every few seconds. He was holding back.

Tears ran down her cheeks. 'Oh, darling, take your pleasure inside me, give it to me—I need it...'

She saw him letting go, letting his agonised ecstasy show. He *had* been waiting for her permission!

'Sherazad...' He arched and drove into her, her name

a lusty growl, convulsing with pleasure, filling her with his seed.

For a long, long time they lay merged, aftershocks of pleasure still rocking them. Finally, careful not to disturb their fusion, he sprawled her over him and hugged her tight.

She lay on top of him, and drowned in the most satisfying sleep of her life. Seconds before she did, she murmured in his throat, 'So *this* is sex!'

She thought she heard him say, 'Not to my knowledge...'

'We'll escort you to your base, then take your patients to Central,' the American commander said as they watched their patients being loaded onto the medical helicopter, while his regiment dismantled and packaged the camp.

'I'd rather it was the other way around,' was Lorenzo's tight response.

The soldier shook his head. 'We have our orders, Dr Banducci.'

Sherazad felt Lorenzo about to tell the man what to do with his orders. She put her hand on his arm, found his muscles bunched. 'Lorenzo! Dean and McFadden are waving to us.'

Lorenzo raised an intimidating eyebrow. He was onto her diversion tactics. He threw a last corrosive glare at the departing commander's indifferent back, then turned on her.

'You think we're dispensable now?'

'You think we're not?' she countered gently. Lorenzo was taking separation from their charges way too badly. 'They have competent doctors and medics with them. Short of being shot out of the air, nothing's going to happen to them. You were absolutely right about not moving them earlier, but now you're being...' She groped for a suitable word.

He supplied it, growled, 'Unreasonable?'

'Why, yes, Dr Brutal Triage!' She nudged him affectionately, and suddenly his hard gaze gentled, then melted, reflecting each and every heated memory of the night and early morning. Then just as suddenly he dragged her to him, and drowned her in the most erotically explicit kiss, right in front of everyone.

She was shocked. She heard the wolf whistles and the laughter. Yet she still turned into a clinging mass of instant yearning.

It was him who withdrew to groan, 'How's that for unreasonable?'

'A fine show of total lack of discretion, old chap.' Ben slapped Lorenzo on the back as he went to board their helicopter. 'And the only bright spot in our grey existence in a long, long time. Do keep it up.'

'My pleasure.' Lorenzo tossed him the nonchalant answer, then added for Sherazad's ears only, 'My almost unendurable pleasure.'

He nearly had to carry her to their patients after that.

They parted with them, among promises on their side to keep updated on their progress, and promises on the soldiers' side never to forget them and to keep in touch. As they finally boarded their helicopter, Sherazad wondered which promises life would allow them to keep.

Two hours later, they were nearing GAO headquarters. Lorenzo came back from talking on the radio and shouted over the rotors' din. 'There'll be a delay in our refugee camp plans. The arrangements I thought I'd made haven't gone through. I'll have to run around quite a bit to get things moving.'

'What are we supposed to do meanwhile?' Emilio shouted back.

Derek shot him a quizzical glance. 'As if we ever lack occupation.'

'Maybe we'll be running around with Lorenzo.' Gulnar sounded so eager that Sherazad bristled. What *did* it take to stop the woman drooling all over him?

It was gratifying to hear Lorenzo's neutral answer. 'No, you won't. I want you to get as much rest as you can. I expect some really tough times ahead.'

Sherazad's alarm rose. 'What about you? You're the least fit among us...'

'Really?' The word was not shouted, yet she was certain everyone had heard—and understood. His mischievously intimate expression said it all anyway, bringing back memories of his fitness, setting her aflame...

She struggled to continue as if he hadn't interrupted her. 'So either you rest too, or take us with you!'

'You can come if you like.'

If she liked? What did he think?

'All of us?' That was enthusiastic Gulnar again.

'No, just Sherazad.' He looked at the men, challenging them to comment. He only got broad, acknowledging smiles.

After that, each pair put their heads back together so they wouldn't shout themselves hoarse. And Lorenzo pulled her onto his lap.

'Is this shock therapy to cure me of any remaining prudish tendencies?' she spluttered.

'This is me being shockingly unable to keep my hands off you after weeks of self-imposed torture.' His mouth opened on her pulse. A second later he withdrew sharply, his face anxious. 'But if it bothers you...'

It didn't. Not in the least. In fact, she couldn't even contemplate wasting one moment of intimacy with him on account of so-called propriety. He'd set her free. And she loved him for it.

She loved him anyway. In every way.

There, she'd admitted it.

It seemed he misinterpreted her rapt stare. '*Dio*, what an unthinking—' She intercepted his agitated words in her mouth, showing him her equal unashamed hunger. He sagged with relief, then responded immediately, taking over the kiss.

She drew away enough to gulp, 'How's *that* for unthinking?'

Lorenzo's eyes flared and he looked about to say things

that would scorch her down to her toes when the pilot's voice crackled over the com system.

'You're in time for an emergency, folks. They just brought in a news crew that got caught in the crossfire in the latest hostilities. Doesn't sound good.'

Lorenzo lurched then seemed to turn to stone beneath her. Alarm kicked inside her. She cupped his face in trembling hands.

'Lorenzo, what is it? Are you afraid it's someone you know?'

But it seemed his sight and hearing had turned inside to whatever personal nightmare had him in its grip. He kissed her absently, then set her off his lap and went to talk to the pilot.

She turned frantic eyes to the others who'd known him longer.

It was Emilio who supplied the missing piece in Lorenzo's puzzle. 'Seven years ago, Lorenzo's brother Piero was an embedded reporter with NATO forces. He got seriously injured, chest and abdomen, in an ambush. He was operated on in an army hospital, but as they were inundated, and independent aid operations were inadequate, he had to be flown back home. Prematurely. He barely made it there. He died in Lorenzo's arms.'

CHAPTER NINE

'How long was Mr Csagoly trapped under the rubble?' Sherazad asked the paramedic who'd brought in her casualty.

He hung a saline bag up. 'I just know it's been an hour since we got him out.'

'Four and a half hours...' Mr Csagoly wheezed the answer, and Sherazad's eyes snapped to him.

She'd already exchanged the basic information about his case with the paramedic—his name and vitals, mechanism of injury and basic emergency measures undertaken. The man was outwardly uninjured, but he was deteriorating right in front of her eyes. A diagnosis was already forming in her mind. His answer didn't reassure her.

'I'm Dr Dawson, Mr Csagoly. Can move your legs?'

'B-barely, but...hurts, more every second...' He paused to snatch a laboured breath. 'The others... Tanya went out to Mikhael—was shot down too. Are they dead?'

Even if she'd known, Sherazad wouldn't have told him. She cast a quick look to where Lorenzo and other doctors were fighting to stabilise their own patients. 'Whatever their injuries, they're in the best hands. Let's take care of you now.' She turned to the paramedic. 'Full exposure, and another BP reading while I examine him.'

Minutes later, her diagnosis reinforced, she was about to begin new emergency measures when the paramedic was called away to a new casualty situation.

Sherazad called out for assistance. Gulnar rushed to her side in seconds—and Lorenzo.

'I only need Gulnar, Lorenzo...' She trailed off. If he was here, his casualties had been beyond help.

The blue tinge to his face confirmed it. Then his subdued words. 'Daniel's handling the depressed skull fracture. Rajeef has the vascular injury. I got the two with multiple chest and abdominal trauma—too late this time. So I have nothing to do.'

Her heart kicked sickeningly, compassion for him swamping her. She finally understood why he'd derailed his life and relinquished his success. Understood his driven intensity, his going way beyond the call of duty, even endangering himself to save his patients. He was striving to save the brother he hadn't been there for in every person injured in a war.

And now he'd lost two more people, in unbearably similar circumstances. She felt the agony he could barely suppress. Answering agony rose inside her.

But she couldn't afford to focus on anything but her patient. The man had a potentially lethal condition.

She turned to Gulnar. 'Gulnar, saline-glucose instead of Ringer's lactate, three litres over two hours then a litre every two hours. Catheterise, Foley's catheter, and hook to a cardiac monitor.'

Gulnar documented her treatments then expertly implemented them. She gave Sherazad a significant glance. 'BP 80 over 50, pulse 40.'

Mr Csagoly was slipping deeper in shock. Sherazad eyed the collecting urine. Brown. This was another proof. 'There's myoglobin in the urine. Test for amount and alert me if urine output is less than 300 cc an hour, or less than 6.5 pH. We need to flush that myoglobin out, force the kidney to excrete it—so infuse twenty per cent mannitol. Also 50 mEq bicarbonate to each litre of saline-glucose to keep urine alkaline. Draw two tubes of blood.'

Sherazad added a list of the tests she wanted as she placed the central venous catheter needed to guide fluid infusion and monitor central blood pressure.

Lorenzo concluded his exam of Mr Csagoly's swollen, tense limbs. 'Did they splint your legs on the way, sir?'

'No…' Mr Csagoly gasped, more disoriented by the second. 'They said nothing was broken…'

Lorenzo's face remained neutral, but she felt his disappointment. It meant he'd reached the same diagnosis.

He took her aside. 'Your diagnosis?'

'Crush injury to both legs and buttocks.'

He nodded. 'No splinting only released more fluid into his injured limbs, and more myoglobin from them into his circulation.'

It wasn't any comfort, having her diagnosis confirmed. 'What's worse, he's almost out of the six-hour window after which both dehydration and high myoglobin concentrations cause irreversible kidney damage.'

Lorenzo's expression got darker. 'Hopefully, your aggressive measures will prevent that.'

Sherazad hoped so too. But crush syndrome, or traumatic rhabdomyolysis, was a silent killer. At first most patients had no complaints, but shortly after extrication they deteriorated and died, giving the syndrome its name of 'rescue death'. Crushed muscles absorbed huge amounts of fluid from the blood, decreasing its volume, leading to severe dehydration. Blood pressure fell rapidly, leading to shock that could quickly become irreversible.

Complicating that, the crushed muscles' contents escaped into the circulation. Myoglobin, or muscle haemoglobin, if not flushed out with aggressive fluid resuscitation and diuretics within six hours, caused acute renal failure that would either be fatal or, at best, lead to lifelong dependence on dialysis. The escaping potassium caused death from cardiac arrest.

'Blood pressure and pulse improving.' Lorenzo turned his eyes from the monitor to her. 'Urine output is too. Your measures are working.'

She shook her head. 'They're only stabilising his general condition. Even that's not certain until sixty hours have passed. But look at his legs. He's developing compartment syndrome—he'll need extensive fasciotomy.'

Lorenzo looked sceptical. 'I've done fasciotomies, just not in crush injuries, so I've no precedent. Those against it say that turning a closed injury into an extensive open wound by surgical intervention means a much higher infection risk to the already injured muscles. In his compromised condition, that's life-threatening. Maybe we'd better go for supportive measures and hope it will resolve. If it's a choice between limb and life…'

She shook her head again, more vigorously this time. 'It won't be. We once treated twenty-six train accident casualties with the syndrome back home. In selected and timely cases, patients survived and kept their limbs, with better than expected function. I have every faith in the procedure's safety and benefits.'

His eyes stilled on hers for a long moment. Then he nodded and instructed Gulnar to arrange for immediate surgery. Sherazad's heart missed a few beats.

Lorenzo trusted her judgement! Just like that! Fastidious, loath-to-relegate Lorenzo was depending on her skill and opinion more and more every day. It was one of her life's greatest privileges—and responsibilities.

With her heart still dropping beats, still savouring the pleasure and pride of his professional esteem, she returned to her patient, injecting him with a massive loading dose of antibiotics and a tetanus toxoid.

'Mr Csagoly, we'll have to operate…'

The drowsy man's eyes rounded in horror. 'You'll…cut off my legs?'

Sherazad interrupted his terrified gasping. 'No, no. The procedure is to *prevent* that. Right now, your tissues are swelling so much they're closing your arteries. Without blood or oxygen, your muscles and nerves are dying. That's why your pain is increasing and you can't move or feel your legs properly. The fasciotomy Dr Banducci will perform will cut through the tissues covering your muscles to relieve the building pressure, so that circulation resumes and no further injury occurs.'

Mr Csagoly digested her information with apparent difficulty. He had only one thing to ask. 'Will I…walk again?'

Lorenzo answered him this time, placing a supporting hand on his arm. 'We'll do everything, and I mean *everything*, to ensure the best possible result.'

Mr Csagoly clung to Lorenzo's hand and closed his eyes on a despairing groan. Sherazad was ready with a diazepam injection, sedating him.

Gulnar came rushing back, calling out, 'All set.' They released the brakes on his trolley bed and raced to Theatre.

Two hours later, they walked out after what a stiff Lorenzo called a 'satisfactory' procedure.

Sherazad's heart bled at his despondency. She was about to try to coax him out of it when they were ambushed by a group of his colleagues and dragged to the restaurant of the three-level ski-resort turned medical facility for a celebration of their safe return.

To her surprise Lorenzo immediately turned on his sunny persona and introduced her to three dozen people, whose names she promptly forgot. He soon had them choking on their food and drink with anecdotes about his kidnapping and kidnappers, turning the horrific experience into a mine of dark but hilarious humour. The gathering went on in a general atmosphere of elation, until two hours later he finally rose and tugged her to her feet.

'We'd better call it a night before we need stomach lavage. *Grazie, mi amici*, it's good to be back.'

He nearly ran all the way to his room on the upper floor, and Sherazad ran after him, laughing her excitement at his impatience to have her alone again. She felt the same. And how!

But as she entered the room, everything inside her dimmed. The former luxury room was…dismal. It had been stripped bare, no doubt by looting, of even the glued-down carpeting, only a utilitarian double bed covered in hospital whites occupying its wide expanse. Lorenzo's personal ef-

fects were crammed in boxes. His few clothes hung on a
wall that bore witness to the ravages of war. He whirled her
around and, mercifully, her mind emptied of all but him.
She was eagerly expecting his bone-melting smile. What she
saw instead... Her ready smile faltered. 'Lorenzo—'

He caught her words in a savage mouth that would have
forced her lips open had they not parted willingly. He bit
them, his tongue plunging deep inside her, driving in furious
rhythms, draining her of every drop of sweetness, growling
for more. It was too much—too *stimulating*. He transferred
his teeth to her neck and she cried out.

'Scared?' He pressed her hard to the wall and bore down
on her with his full formidable weight.

She understood. He was seeking refuge from anguish and
helplessness in unrestrained passion. And how she craved
to accommodate him. Melting in his grip, she gave herself
over to him. 'I was never scared of you, darling. Not even
when I mistook you for a murderer.'

In answer to her trusting words, he growled and lifted her
off the floor. Her heartbeats spilled all over the place in
thrilled awe at his effortless strength. His large hands spread
her legs around his hips, then he thrust his erection at the
junction of her thighs, almost entering her through their
clothes.

She moaned her surrender and his eyes blazed. 'You
weren't scared because I was nice and gentle. I don't feel
nice and gentle any more. I won't be. Scared now?'

She should be. She'd suffered at the hands of an out-of-
control man before. But Lorenzo would never be out of
control. Even now, he was still asking her permission to let
go, and no matter what power she gave him over her, she
knew he'd never abuse it.

She wound herself around him tighter, giving him fuller
access to her core. Pleasure and anticipation almost knocked
her out. 'You don't scare me, Lorenzo.'

'Only because you don't know what I want to do to you.'
He rubbed up and down her body in abandon, accentuating

every fierce word with a thrust and a bite, until she was almost weeping with arousal. 'How many ways I want to take you—*take you*—Sherazad!'

She'd die if he didn't. Oh, why wasn't he doing it already? Barely able to open eyes heavy with craving, she met his feverish gaze. 'You always promise what you don't deliver, darling?' She didn't recognise the throaty, greedy voice as she teased him with his own words from all those weeks ago. 'Show me, Lorenzo. Take me every way you want.'

He rumbled deep in his gut and dropped her to her feet, then dropped to his knees, dragging her jeans off with barely contained force. He didn't even remove his, just freed himself. Her heart slowed, each beat a thunderclap, as if her blood had thickened, needing a much more powerful contraction to push it though her veins. Then she was airborne, wrapped around his steel buttocks, and he rammed inside her with one savage thrust, sinking into her empty, cramping flesh to the hilt.

She died of pleasure.

Then she lived again, but only when he set her heart beating to the frenzied tempo of his thrusts inside her. She convulsed around him inside and out. Her cries blurred into a continuous wail of agonised ecstasy, echoing his roars.

He drove deeper into her clinging resistance, until she felt the great pulse of pleasure tighten, the heat focused in her loins desperate for one more stoke to burst into the inferno that would consume her, re-create her. He gave it to her, and they exploded together. He fed her convulsions with climactic rams, slamming her to the wall, jetting inside her, taking her to complete quivering fulfilment.

Still buried inside her, he kept murmuring in Italian how she almost killed him with too much pleasure, claiming her swollen, satisfied lips in abandon.

Then he suddenly jolted away as if she'd shot him again. Without his support, her satiation-drained legs buckled and she sank to the floor in confusion.

Lorenzo staggered back and fell on the bed, her tears burning his lips. He'd hurt her! He'd been half-crazed with revisited grief. He'd needed to drown in her, hide inside her, erase with her passion and compassion all the ugliness and the pain and the desperation.

And she'd offered it all, so generously, so eagerly.

But she'd wanted him to take her, not attack her!

He watched her unique features darkening and his heart convulsed.

'I'm no better than Jack, am I?' He could barely speak, his body shaking with a mixture of satisfaction and horror. 'Just another stupid, selfish male after his own gratification. And I wanted to kill him, for what he did to you!'

She gaped at him.

Then she burst out laughing, and it was his turn to gape.

'Stupid? You're *too* intelligent, though you do have your dumb moments where I'm concerned. And selfish? This sated-out-of-her-mind-and-begging-for-more woman begs to differ. As for that sorry bastard, he's not worth one drop of your attention. Save it all for me!'

He shook his head, confused, elation hovering at the edge of his mind, scared to enter. 'But you're crying…'

'Ecstatic tears, you silly man.' She sat back on her heels and slowly stripped off her shirt, her smile leaving him in no doubt that she meant every word. Then she approached him on all fours, like a sinuous cat seeking her mate. She came between his legs, slowly removed his trousers then rubbed her silken body against his hair-roughened flesh.

He fell back on the bed and surrendered to her as she indulged her every whim, his mind lost, everything else hers. At last she looked up from loving him and pouted. 'You promised to take me in every way!'

So for the rest of the night, he did.

'I still can't believe this!'

Sherazad's frown deepened at Lorenzo's soft chuckle. She turned to glare at him as he manoeuvred along the picturesque forest road to Zvetnia, the nearby town harbouring the Badovnans' provisional government.

What was there to chuckle about? For the last month she'd followed him around the region as he negotiated his heart out with every faction of influence to obtain security for aid convoys' arrival in the region and their path to the camp. She'd been stunned and enraged by the obstacle-creating attitudes of all those in power.

'Sherazad, save yourself a perpetual headache and heart-ache and just believe that no one's anxious to solve our difficulties.'

'But why? I expected that from the Azernians, but they were the most helpful, saying they'll do everything they can to control rogue factions sabotaging humanitarian efforts!'

'They want to win international opinion points by playing the saints. While every faction's agendas have become so tangled, it's futile trying to make sense of anything. So let's just concentrate on our jobs.'

She huffed a frustrated exhalation. 'At least we've reached the easy part. The Badovnans will surely give us all the help they can.'

Lorenzo tossed her a cynical look, and she exclaimed, 'What? The camp is populated by their own people!'

'Think about it, Sherazad. This is a propaganda war, as well as a physical one. The worse off their people are, the more international sympathy they'll garner for their cause, strengthening their claims for independence, maybe extending their borders as well.'

'That's horrible!'

'That's life.'

'You mean that's politics.'

'Whatever—that's how things are.'

'Then it's possible *they* kidnapped you and attacked my convoy, to make the Azernians look barbarous, to score more points against them!'

'We might never know for sure, but anything's possible—and plausible.'

'That's horrible.'

'Repeating yourself, *mia amore*?' His gentle hand smoothed her hot cheek. She turned her lips in his palm. 'It *is* horrible—atrocious…'

'And you haven't seen the camp yet.'

She flinched and he groaned and tugged her to him. She surged into his embrace, shutting out everything else but him. And the way he called her his love, so sensually—so convincingly.

He buried soft kisses in her hair: 'We'll make it better. Everyone who cares makes a difference. People like you make it all worth fighting for, make life worth living.'

Suddenly, every feeling she had for him flared out of control. 'And people like you. Lorenzo, darling. I want you—please, *now*!'

Sherazad's passionate, desperate appeal dragged out his instantaneous reaction, the perpetual hunger simmering at skin level, waiting to burst into an inferno at the merest whisper, look or touch.

He drove the Jeep off the road and deep under the forest's cover. The second he turned off the engine, he reached for her, merging with her in a frenzied kiss, one she met with equal power.

After that time he'd taken her hard and fast, he'd tried to return to slow and gentle. She'd made it impossible, telling him just being near him had her constantly aroused, to just love her, show her the full force of his passion, never waste a moment of their time together.

Now was another such moment to be wrung out of time, another piece of heaven to be snatched out of the clutches of hell. No matter what.

Never breaking the kiss, he reached under her skirt—wondering for a split second if she'd worn one today with this in mind—and dragged down her thick pantyhose and panties. The Jeep would soon chill so he couldn't risk taking off more of her clothes. She helped him frantically as he swung one of her legs over his shoulder and the other on the dashboard, offering him the best access to her. He was starting to shake and so was she.

'Hurry…' Her moan had him clawing at his zipper. He managed to work it around his arousal, then wrapped one cushioning arm around her back, the other behind her head, so he wouldn't slam her into the door.

'It'll be uncomfortable,' he panted.

'I don't care.' She dragged him to her. He sank into her with the jarring momentum of his lunge. He lurched, shouted as her molten heat absorbed him. He stilled inside her, buried deep, revelling in her domination, his captivation. Then the scent of her desire, the sound of her pleasure and the sight of her face, transfigured by ecstasy, drove him on.

But he was too viciously aroused. A few unbridled thrusts would finish him. Mercifully, she was as far gone, already screaming his name and spasming. He thrust her over the edge then threw himself after her.

A long time later, they were back on the road, still caressing and murmuring their lingering pleasure.

'You shouldn't have done that, *mia amore*.' He sighed as he savoured the magnificent feel and scent of her, swirled her taste in his mouth. 'Now I have no tension, no aggression left to handle those creeps.'

She nuzzled his neck. 'I didn't see you fighting me off.'

'When you use your weapons of mass destruction? The night in your eyes, heaven in your body and madness in your passion? What chance have I got, a mere mortal?'

'Well, if you want your tension restored…' She bit his earlobe, a naughty hand slipping beneath his sweater, the other to his distending manhood.

By the time they reached their destination, he was ready to take on a battalion of Badovnan militia in hand-to-hand combat.

'I can't believe we're finally heading to the camp,' Gulnar said brightly as she passed around sandwiches.

They were all squashed together in the back of their least-packed supplies-filled truck, with local volunteers driving their convoy to spare them the exhaustion of the ten-hour drive. Lorenzo had ended up between Gulnar and Sherazad. As the former handed him his food, she pressed her sizeable breasts into him. He nearly shoved her away, his gaze involuntarily darting to Emilio's clenching jaw.

He hated to think what Sherazad must be thinking, feeling. Not that she'd ever commented, in any way, on Gulnar's blatant behaviour. He marvelled at her restraint. If it had been the other way around, he would have pulverised the man pursuing her. But she probably didn't care because it was something he didn't invite and tried his best to stop.

Or maybe she just doesn't care who else gets you, a corrosive voice inside his head sneered, *because she doesn't care about you. Like every other woman you've met on the frontline, like Gulnar...*

He smothered the voice.

'You make it sound as if we're going to summer camp, Gulnar!' Emilio nearly snatched his food from her hand.

Gulnar's green eyes flashed. '*I* lived in a refugee camp once, if you remember!'

'Now, now, children.' Ben intervened in his usual even-tempered way. 'Save all that energy for what lies ahead.'

Gulnar and Emilio looked away, livid color staining both faces, and Lorenzo almost groaned. This was no longer the seamless team he'd worked so hard to build. Gulnar was almost outrageous, Emilio almost hostile, the others awkward.

Not that he could blame Emilio. Loving a woman who was worthy of love, apart from this aberration, must be hell.

He imagined himself in Emilio's shoes, with Sherazad ignoring him and pursuing another man, a friend, right under his eyes... He instinctively hugged her tighter to his side.

'Any more news from the camp?' Sherazad spoke for the first time. She'd been dozing in his embrace for most of the seven hours since they'd left GAO Headquarters, only waking up when they'd proposed having lunch. He'd kept her up all night. Only fair—she'd kept him up, in every way....

He blinked back the images of their mating in the last shower they'd have in a long time, and latched onto the professional opening she provided. 'Only those I got this morning, changing everything. The refugees have doubled to sixty thousand after the outbreak of hostilities, with as many expected over the next few weeks.'

At their collective gasp he went on. 'That's not all. The former clinic, such as it was, has been shut down and they've been without medical care for a month. We'll have to set up a clinic from scratch. Kinear's and Olafson's teams are already setting up the new shelters, water-supply systems and latrines, but they'll probably need our help once we've set up our working and living quarters.'

Derek's idealistic temperament flared. 'And the powers that be left it to the last moment to tell us all that, huh? What did they think? That we'd back down if we knew the real size of the job?'

Lorenzo shook his head. 'You're crediting them with premeditation, Derek, when it's all lack of intelligence, co-ordination and plain caring.'

'Total chaos, eh?' Sherazad exhaled.

'Exactly.'

Three hours of uneasy silence later, interspersed with edgy side-conversations, they arrived at their destination.

Lorenzo jumped out of the truck first and stretched up both arms to help her down. Sherazad went eagerly into his powerful arms, her heart spilling in her intimate smile. Then she gazed beyond his head—and froze.

She vaguely felt him carrying her down, the others following, all pausing as they took in the humanitarian catastrophe. But soon they were unloading the truck, leaving only her, the novice among them, still paralysed by what she saw.

For as far as she could see, on a now grassless meadow, lay ragged rows of flimsy tents, flailing in the brutal

February wind. Enough people to fill two stadiums, a huge percentage of them women and children in colourful tatters, were huddled together in endless queues at food and water outlets and latrines. Most of them turned to watch them, their eyes a heart-wrenching mixture of expectation and despondence.

This was beyond chaos—beyond desolation.

But she was not there to feel sorry and horrified. She was there to do something about it. Forcing herself out of her trance, she focused on Lorenzo's words.

'…with vaccinations. There are about eight thousand children below five. Gulnar, Emilio, arrange a schedule with the camp leaders. Ben, Derek, set up our quarters. Sherazad and I will set up the clinic. OK, go.'

Lorenzo turned to her and she looked up at him. 'I thought I understood—could imagine…'

Instant understanding flooded his eyes. He smoothed her hair behind her ear. 'Seeing it for real *is* jarring.'

She clung to his hand as if she'd find a reason within his grasp, something to make it all more acceptable. 'And this could happen to anyone, anywhere. A war could break out, and with little or no warning anyone could find themselves fleeing for their lives, ending up in a place like this…'

He nodded. 'Or worse! There *are* worse conditions in the world. Though this is bad enough with the brutal winter. On the last estimates I got this morning, there's a tent for every twelve people, a rations outlet for every two thousand, a tap for every thousand and a latrine for every two hundred. That's four to five times more than the minimum acceptable standard for health and sanitation. But we're here, and we'll make it better.'

When she remained stiff, wondering what fifty or so people could really do, he hugged her fiercely, then nudged her into step with him. 'You'll feel better when you're being useful.'

'Gulnar, where's that DPT injection?'

Sherazad pressed down hard on her flaring temper. If

not as hard as four-year-old Arjan's teeth had sunk into her hand.

She'd used up her limited Badovnan, and the passive woman supposedly holding him for her was no help at all. She wasn't his mother. Not even a relative. The pale, blond boy was among the hundreds of children found wandering alone after they'd been separated from their kin in the war.

She'd dropped the polio vaccine down his throat, and was reasonably sure he'd swallowed before he'd begun spitting in her face. She'd injected him with the measles and the meningitis Haemophilus Influenzae B vaccines. All that remained was the diphtheria-pertussis—whooping cough and tetanus combined vaccine. *If* she could convince him she wasn't trying to kill him.

'Here!' Gulnar stumbled over to her, pushing the syringe into her hand. They were both near collapse. For the past two weeks, they'd been working in teams of two for ten hours every day, vaccinating the children. Then there were the other endless medical chores, helping setting up more shelters and latrines and distributing the donations Lorenzo had accumulated.

'I know you don't believe it's for your own good, but...' Sherazad hated exerting her strength on the fragile boy's arm, but it was that or break the needle in it. Afterwards, he ran out, still screaming like an ambulance siren. She sighed and filled in his vaccination card.

Gulnar flopped on the chair beside her. 'Our last patient won't come in without his mother and she had to go to the bathroom. Then we're out of vaccines. What will we do about the three thousand-plus arrivals? Derek said he has two measles cases.'

'That's all we need!' Sherazad let her head drop to the table with a thunk. Measles, while not too serious in optimum health conditions, was the number one killer of children in situations like this. Without vaccinations an outbreak could prove disastrous. 'Lorenzo is doing all he can.'

Their last patient came in. They dragged themselves up, falling into the routine. But this time they wished for a screaming child or a hysterical mother. Even a measles outbreak would have been preferable.

In minutes, Sherazad left Gulnar carrying out resuscitation and ran to alert Lorenzo. She entered the other clinic tent to find him growling into his mobile. '...precautions for the convoy's safety. I need those vaccines and I need them now!'

The person on the other side growled back and Lorenzo listened in apparent frustration. Sherazad whispered to Emilio about their situation and he promptly ran out to help Gulnar.

Realising she was there, Lorenzo turned and held out an eager hand. She rushed to him, loving how he'd come to depend on her, even if all she could do was just be there. He pressed her to his side, ending the conversation on a taut, 'I expect a meeting time and place tomorrow.'

'We'll go fetch our supplies?' she asked gently.

'*I'll* go!'

'Fat chance.' He opened his mouth to persist and she silenced him with a kiss. Then she gave him her news. 'We've got our first case of cholera.'

Shock rippled through him, transmitting itself back to her. She hugged him tighter.

'It could be something else!'

She shook her head in regret. 'Something else with painless, rice-water diarrhoea, fishy odour, no fever, vomiting, dehydration within an hour, and in our compromised sanitation conditions? She's my last vaccination patient's mother. I gave her ORS, but I think she'll need IV fluids soon.'

He squeezed his eyes. 'Tell me you've been obsessive in your sterile technique!'

The first thing he cared about was that she hadn't been infected. She nodded, too overcome to answer.

He sighed in relief. 'As for me, my ulcer will protect me.'

She knew the high acid content of the stomach associated with an ulcer killed the *Vibrio cholerae* bacterium, protecting those with ulcers from infection. 'You don't have an ulcer!'

'I'm developing one as we speak. Come, *amore*. Let's see how bad this really is!'

It was catastrophic.

Within two days a full-blown epidemic had manifested. Dozens then hundreds fell ill. And no matter how fast they dealt with one wave of cases, another wave came along, nearly deluging them.

Lorenzo's roars for proper sanitation were at last heeded now the whole region was in imminent danger of a sweeping epidemic. There were no new cases, but that didn't mean much for those already suffering. Older people and children were hit hardest, going into severe dehydration and shock faster than others.

Every able-bodied aid worker and refugee helped. But it was still overwhelming.

Day and night merged and time turned to limbo as they ran around, boiling water, resuscitating shocked patients, administering ORS—the WHO oral rehydration solution that contained the salts, sugars and minerals the body lost profusely—to all those who could drink, and intravenous fluids to those who couldn't. Then IV fluids ran out and they resorted to giving ORS via the nasogastric route.

Dozens deteriorated in spite of their best efforts and needed intensive-care measures. No one could help their core team with those. By the end of three weeks, when they at last got medical relief, from volunteers pulled from other aid services and local medical personnel, they were all beyond exhaustion.

Eight weeks after the beginning of the epidemic, the last patients were on their way to recovery.

'Do you always have to be right?'

They'd just finished their evening rounds and were heading back to the kitchen tent, with Lorenzo supporting Sherazad's staggering body in the curve of his.

'You mean I created the epidemic by diagnosing it?' Her attempted laugh was knocked out of her when she stumbled. He caught her, barely. He wasn't steady on his feet either. 'And *always* right? You once thought I knew nothing.'

His grimace was all indulgence. 'I never thought that. I only wish you'd been wrong this time.'

'A first-year medical student would have recognised the classical clinical picture. But at least we beat it, got our sanitation fixed...'

'After eight people died.'

Afterwards, they swayed the rest of the way in silence. Losing patients was something they'd never come to terms with.

As soon as they entered the tent, Derek, Ben and Emilio jumped on Lorenzo with questions and reports. Sherazad found herself alone with Gulnar as they made hot drinks. And curiosity finally got the best of her.

'You know, Gulnar, I really like you. But why are you doing this?'

Gulnar didn't even pretend to misunderstand. 'I've been without a man since my fiancé was killed in our war. Then I was in the refugee camp—but let's not go there. Since then...' She made an expressive gesture at their conditions.

Sherazad could sympathise. But she still didn't understand. 'So why not Emilio? You *are* attracted to him, and he cares deeply for you.'

For the first time, Sherazad saw an intense emotion darkening Gulnar's radiant features. She snapped an agitated glance at Emilio. 'That's exactly why I push him away. Caring for someone when they could be blown to bits tomorrow is not only stupid, it's suicide—slow suicide!'

Sherazad finally understood, deeply, painfully. If not completely. 'Then why Lorenzo? *My* lover?'

Gulnar shrugged nonchalantly. 'Because he's not really

your lover, just your sex partner. Because he's safe. Everyone knows about him. With him, it's always just sex. He cares about the big issues, but on the personal level he's incapable of caring—about me, or about you.'

CHAPTER TEN

'So, YOU don't care?'

Lorenzo watched as Sherazad rose to her knees beside him on their spartan tent's floor. Wearing only his open shirt, she struck a mouthwatering pose as she tried to gauge his sincerity.

'Not in the slightest.' He let her see what she did to him, reclining in the way that always drove her crazy with passion. Her lips parted, her breath came in quick puffs and her eyes—*those eyes*—took him on a graphic tour where her desires raged. But she held back, kept her hands to herself.

'I'm calling your bluff, big man.' She wasn't playing fair. She knew he couldn't stand it for long when she sounded like that, looked at him like that. He felt his control slipping.

'I'll take that as a compliment.' Great! Now she must feel it too. He'd intended a confident, seductive whisper, not this wavering moan.

'That's huge of you.' Her soft innuendo rushed to every erogenous zone in his body. It never failed. Every time she put her sharp wit to such erotic use his wonder grew, as did his appreciation. Every time she lost another shred of inhibition with him, his delight surged. Five months ago, he hadn't known she existed. Now he couldn't imagine existence without her. Five months—had it really been five months already? 'But you're not distracting me. Either you tell me or, if you really don't care, you'll give the camp something they'll cherish to their dying day. The sight of your fully exposed magnificence. You can make it at a run. I don't want you catching cold.'

Dio, but she exhilarated him! His reserved Sherazad, who'd once blushed and squirmed at his tame-in-comparison Q and A, was embroiling him in an outrageous game of Truth or Dare.

He'd played along. He'd told her the truth sometimes, taken her delicious dares at others. Until that last question. No way was he answering it. Or taking that dare. It was time he rewrote the rules.

He surged towards her and she met him halfway. They fell on the bedding, already joined, already driving towards the ultimate satisfaction. This wasn't the first time—or the second—tonight, yet their hunger was still too sharp and soon they were convulsing in each other's arms, dissolving in heat and closeness, their pleasure complete.

She lay under him, containing him and clinging to him as if he was all she needed. He clung back, deepening their merging, praying it was really so.

'I'm on to you.' This wasn't fair. Just one whisper and he started simmering again. 'This was so you wouldn't take up my dare.'

'This was so I wouldn't have a stroke.' He bent to her breasts, slaking the hunger he'd forgone in the frenzy, savouring the music of her pleasure.

She returned the sensual onslaught, stroking and tasting him, tightening around him. Then from a receding reality he heard her gasp, 'We'll make love ten times then you'll still give me the dare or the truth.'

'I'll give you anything, *mia amore*, always…' And he would too.

She stopped her caresses in anticipation.

'Don't stop! All right—*yes*, a man made a pass at me once!'

'He propositioned you?' She was all attention now.

'I don't acknowledge pick-ups any more than you do…' *Per Dio*, what was he saying? Now he'd never hear the end of this.

'You mean you're accustomed to them?' She burst out in howls of laughter.

There was only one way to shut her up.

Afterwards, as they lay replete and nerveless, wrapped around each other, she still chuckled in his neck. 'Can't blame the poor guy...'

Sherazad stirred to find Lorenzo disentangling himself from her arms. It was totally dark outside. Her limbs and head each weighed a delicious ton, but she still tried to move, to join him in whatever crisis he'd been called to. He stopped her with a soft kiss. 'It's nothing I can't take care of alone. Sleep, *amore*.'

In seconds he was dressed and out of the tent.

Sleep, *amore*, he'd said. But sleep had evaporated now she no longer had his reassuring heartbeat to lull her. Even with the constant exhaustion of camp life, once he was away from her, warring thoughts and feelings attacked her, making rest or peace impossible.

Every moment she spent alone she relived the shocked anguish her encounter with Gulnar had caused. Saw Gulnar's equal shock at realising that she wasn't like Lorenzo's other frontline women, just seeking psychological release through a temporary sexual liaison with a no-strings-attached Don Juan. That her emotions were fully involved.

Logic said she had no reason to be shocked or anguished. In a way, that was how it had started. Along with her need to prove that Jack had not damaged her for life, she'd been out to discover her femininity and to indulge her unstoppable desire for Lorenzo. There had been no thoughts of what next. And when he'd told her there'd be no 'what next' with him, she hadn't cared. She'd grabbed at the 'now' and clung.

Now she didn't want to ever let go.

But her six months on the frontline were coming to an end.

On one hand, she couldn't wait for the professional experience to end. It might not say much for her as a human being, but being on the frontline was just too much. She still wanted a career in aid work—just not on frontlines.

On the other hand, that was where Lorenzo had pledged to be for the rest of his life. And no matter how she hated the unrelenting desperation and brutality of frontline reality, being with him far outweighed anything else.

That was, if he wanted her with him.

Gulnar had said he didn't. And it wasn't only her. All the others, including him, said that he put all his capacity for caring and commitment into his chosen life path. That he had nothing to invest in a personal relationship.

But she believed it was no longer true. She had to.

For even if their world-shattering intimacies, his constant caring for her well-being and their deepening rapport could be explained by the facts that he was a master sensualist and a compassionate human being, what could explain his faithfulness? The Casanova he was supposed to be wouldn't have turned down an offer like Gulnar's. He wouldn't have thought anything of sharing himself among the females clamouring for his favours.

Granted, they didn't talk about anything beyond the present, but how could they in the chaos they existed in? He didn't talk of what next, but that didn't mean his emotions weren't involved. He wouldn't be this way with her if they weren't, would he?

He cared. She knew it. He wanted their relationship to continue, whatever tomorrow would bring…

She sprang to her feet and into her clothes. She had to see him again, read in his eyes the answers that would banish the doubts that were undermining her soul.

Minutes later, she entered the clinic tent to the sound of his beloved voice singing a local song in broken harmony with a familiar voice. Sure enough, there he was, bent over thirteen-year-old Ashjay's leg, suturing a long, deep gash. Ben had clearly done the anaesthesia and was now assisting.

Lorenzo raised his eyes as soon as she entered, and there it was—everything she needed to feel secure.

She returned his intimate smile, before Ashjay's eager

one made her turn her attention to him. She noticed another tooth missing another piece.

The reckless teenager had become a regular patient ever since he'd arrived at the camp four weeks ago, each time with a different ailment or injury, from minor to life-threatening.

'Want some help?'

Ben took up her offer eagerly. 'Please! I'll put away my regional anaesthesia tray and equipment, and escape. Those two are giving me brain damage with their atrocious singing.'

Lorenzo and Ashjay exchanged a mischievous grin and broke into raucous singing again. Ben groaned and stuffed cotton wool in his ears.

She snapped on gloves, taking the scissors from Ben. As she took her place opposite Lorenzo, they concluded their song on a jagged high note. She stuck her tongue out at both of them, and got her first good look at the ragged wound.

'Ouch.' She winced at the sight of Ashjay's nearly split open calf muscle.

'Got that climbing mountain!' Ashjay announced proudly.

'In the middle of the night?' Sherazad shook her head at his zeal. It owed a great deal to Ben's thorough anaesthesia, but she knew that collecting yet another scar and daredevil story was his driving motivation. As if he needed more strife in his life! But it seemed, in the dehumanising conditions he'd found himself in, Ashjay found his relief and enter-tainment in exposing himself to danger of his own making.

'And he was surprised we were cross with him!' Lorenzo had meticulously closed the muscles, and was now approx-imating the subcutaneous tissues beneath the skin. 'Pass me another Vicryl monofilament strand, *amore*. His tissues mis-behave as much as he does. They take two sutures where one is needed, to agree to come together.'

'I know. I sutured his scalp wound ten days ago. It was uncanny!' She handed him the absorbable catgut thread that would later dissolve inside Ashjay's leg so the sutures wouldn't need removal.

Ben laughed. 'At least he seems to be a disaster magnet. Ever since he arrived, all the accidents and misfortunes happen to him, leaving everything else quiet and running smoothly.'

Lorenzo looked heavenwards in mock long-suffering. 'Haven't you learned never to make remarks like that, Ben? You shouldn't even *think* them! The moment you feel smug and secure—*kerblam*—a string of disasters!'

'I didn't know you were superstitious, Lorenzo.' She gave him a provocative look as she cut the interrupted sutures he'd tied repeatedly, swabbing off excess blood.

'That's not superstition.' He picked up the ready-threaded curved needle and inspected the length of the nylon thread. For skin closure he had to use an unabsorbable material that would remain in place for as long as it took the wound to heal, and would be removed afterwards. 'It's an as yet unexplained law of nature. Like recommendoma!'

'Recommendoma is definitely a medical superstition!' She'd never subscribed to the enduring and widely accepted belief that doctors treating or operating on relatives, loved ones or highly recommended cases always screwed up inexplicably. 'So you are superstitious. Who would have thought it?'

He placed the last suture in what was now a very neat and almost linear repair, and winked at her. 'Your knowledge of me is still not deep enough, then, *tesoro*. I must try harder, intensify your exposure.'

Ashjay, whose English was surprisingly good, looked from one to the other curiously, his bright blue eyes resting on her. No doubt because, for all her new-found bravado, she must be red enough to glow in the dark. 'Is double talk, no?'

Ben sighed. 'It sure is, son. I take it back, folks. It was uplifting once, but watching you two lovebirds is getting depressing. I must talk my ex into giving me another shot as soon as my contract ends.'

At the mention of ending contracts, Sherazad's heart constricted. She darted a glance to witness Lorenzo's reaction. There was none.

He only smiled at Ben, teasing and serious at once. 'If I were a woman, I'd give you a second chance. But I'm glad you're still here for a while yet. Now things are finally under control in the camp, we're heading to Brezny. We've got our work cut out for us, rehabilitating their main hospital and training their local doctors and medics in the newest techniques of medicine and surgery.'

'You have the OK to go there?' This was news to Sherazad. Until a few days ago there'd been serious combat situations around and inside the town.

'Things are under control, as far as the town goes,' Lorenzo said as he wrapped Ashjay's leg in gauze. 'It's the meadows and roads around there that are now the problem. The rebels littered their retreating path with landmines. In fact, our Colonel LaCroix is there now, mine-clearing the region.'

A bolt of cold rage hit her. That someone would leave booby traps that would mutilate or kill thousands of innocents in the haphazard hope of eliminating enemies was beyond heinous. No punishment was enough.

'Are they succeeding?' Her throat closed around the violent emotions.

Lorenzo injected Ashjay with antibiotic and tetanus toxoid cover. 'So far. We'll take the road already declared safe.'

Sherazad recalled something. 'Isn't Brezny where you come from, Ashjay?'

The boy's head bobbed enthusiastically. 'My sister there—cannot leave. I go with you to home. Broke and burned, but home.'

Later, as she once again lay in Lorenzo's arms for the

remaining hours till morning, Ashjay's words echoed in her mind.

Broke and burned, but home.

She'd go back to a safe and luxurious flat and a loving family.

Her home was no longer there.

Home was wherever Lorenzo was.

'You think our replacements will keep the camp running smoothly?'

Lorenzo looked sideways at Sherazad, lost in remembering all the memorable events they'd shared in this very truck. Only Ashjay's presence beside her had kept him from reminiscing with her. He realised she was asking him something, had to replay her question in his mind to make sense of it.

'They were adequate to start with, but now I'm satisfied with their level of competence.' For the last two months they'd trained those who'd needed hands-on experience and updated those who had it. 'They'll be all right.'

'I don't know...' She looked thoughtful—and something more? 'The medics and nurses are all right, but I'd like to continue training the doctors.'

This wasn't the first time she'd wanted to do something that would, of necessity, extend her stay on the frontline beyond her contracted six months. Maybe even indefinitely. It thrilled him, and it oppressed him. He couldn't bear to think she'd leave, yet couldn't bear to think she'd stay.

She'd been spectacular. She'd blended in and had proved to be a superior frontline doctor. But more and more, he felt how draining it was for her. This wasn't what she'd intended to do with the rest of her life. This *shouldn't* be what she did with the rest of her life.

But lately she'd been making overtures, leaving it up to him to expand on the subject. Both professionally and personally, he felt it was his verdict that would make her stay or go.

Professionally, he wanted to beg her to stay. Personally—
Dio! Personally he wanted—he *needed*! For the first time in
his life.

He snatched a longing look at her, sitting there beside
him, animated and heart-rendingly lovely, making Ashjay
giggle. He didn't know what to do, what to say, to make
sure she got what was best for her. He didn't know if it was
fair to tell her how deep his need went...

His thoughts splintered as an explosion ripped the air.

The trucks in front of Lorenzo braked violently, one after
the other. He slammed his foot on the brakes, the sudden
stop forcing the truck to veer sideways. The second it settled
back on its wheels, he lunged over Sherazad and Ashjay,
forcing them into the footwell of the front seat.

'Stay down!' he snarled as he started to slink out of the
truck, keeping low.

Sherazad clung to his arms with rabid strength. 'You're
not getting out!'

'*Déjà vu?*'

'And I'm not letting you go out this time either.'

'Sherazad, I'll just investigate. I'll be careful—'

'No, no, *no*! That's what my driver said, told me to stay
down, before he got out of the truck and was shot dead.
You're staying here.'

The knock on the door made them all jump. It was Derek.

He was relaxed—gloating even. 'Care to give us a hand,
Lor? It's Emilio's tyre. I told him he'd over-inflated it, but
does he ever listen?'

'No bomb?' It was Ashjay who finally found his voice.

Derek's eyes rounded. 'Bomb? Is that what you thought?'

'It's a very plausible assumption, given our circumstances!' Lorenzo snapped, feeling Sherazad's shivering
transmitted to him, shaking him.

The smile died completely on Derek's face as he took in
their positions and Sherazad's ashen colour. 'Oh. Oh, it must
have... With your experience... Oh, I'm sorry...'

Sherazad didn't say anything as Derek gave a helpless shrug and slunk away. Ashjay jumped out and ran after him.

She let go of her vice-like hold on Lorenzo, slumping until her forehead touched the seat, and drew in a sobbing breath. He surged to pull her up and into his arms. He smoothed her hair off her face, planting tender kisses along her cheek and forehead. 'False alarm, *tesoro*.'

She nodded against his chest. 'Go help them. I'll get some tea.'

Her eyes were red with suppressed tears, her breath still catching, her body quivering. His heart almost burst at her distress.

Here was the answer to his uncertainties. He could no longer pretend not to know that the longer she stayed here, the more it got to her. That sooner or later she would break. He had to let her go for her own sake. But could he?

How could he?

Then before his eyes, hers cleared. He felt her relax against him. She pushed herself away, her face brightening as she fetched a pressure gauge and tossed it to him. 'Here, check the rest of Emilio's tyres. I'm not giving him any of our spares!' He laughed yet still looked for pretence, agitation. There was no sign of either as she pinched his buttock. 'I'm also driving when we get going again. That braking was lousy.'

She seemed completely back to normal. Maybe he'd been imagining her stress, being over-solicitous, over-protective. Maybe she *was* cut out to tough out life on frontlines. He felt his mood doing a U-turn, and laughed again, a real laugh this time. 'You never explained your expertise with motor vehicles, *amore*!'

'Easy. Dad owns a trucking business and my brother's a motorcycle freak. Now, get going.' She shoved him out of the truck, sending him on his way with a kiss.

Still chuckling, he jumped down and went to help his team.

In minutes, she followed with an improvised tray and

plastic cups of tea. She giggled at their inexpert struggle with the huge tyre, grilled them a bit, then decided to take pity on them. A few directions later, the tyre was in place and the mystery of operating a pressure gauge was revealed to him at last.

She was halfway back to their truck when she stopped and called out, 'Where's Ashjay?'

'I thought he was back at the truck.'

'No, I…' She stopped, an alarmed look in her eyes. 'Did they clear the meadows or just the roads of landmines?'

His blood froze. Her eyes rounded in horror as she accurately read his. He started to run, but she'd started running first, faster, closer.

Time and space felt as if they'd congealed around him, hindering him. In the slow motion of horrified helplessness, he waded through them, watching her fly towards the boy in the distance. He was poking at something on the ground.

Lorenzo heard her scream as if from an endless tunnel, heard his own frantic shouts scattering into nothingness. Then he heard the explosion, saw the boy fall in a heap to the ground, saw Sherazad freeze in mid-leap, landing on legs that shook for a second before she sank to her knees.

He descended on her the next second, trying to hold her up as she slumped further. His fingers dipped in her hot blood and he lost all co-ordination and power, sagging to her side on a tearing sob. 'Sherazad…*Sherazad*!'

Her blood was everywhere, her eyes scared and uncomprehending. And she still gasped, 'Ashjay… See to Ashjay…'

Heaven help him, he couldn't. Let the others tend the boy. Sherazad was all that mattered.

Emilio fell to his knees beside him. He only noticed him because he had their emergency kit. Lorenzo laid Sherazad back gently, and started to check her with uncontrollably shaking hands. But for a moment both his mind and eyes were blurred with tears, his medical knowledge blotted out by the sight of her blood.

Emilio was already checking her airway. 'Can you breathe on your own? Nod if you can.' She nodded, and he snapped on a rebreather mask and started one hundred per cent oxygen delivery.

Lorenzo finally reacted. 'Emilio, assess circulation!' Then in seconds he'd shredded Sherazad's sleeves and slipped in both arms wide-bore cannulae delivering fluid replacement at the highest rate.

'BP 90 over 60 and falling,' Emilio whispered. 'Very weak distal pulse, especially on the right side, pulse 155.'

Sherazad gasped again, 'Ashjay…'

'The others are taking care of him—just keep your attention with me!' He couldn't control his harshness, but he was going out of his mind with terror, with anger at her for running after the boy. For doing this to herself. 'Can you tell where you're injured?' There was just so much obscuring blood—*Dio*—so much of her precious blood…

Where was it coming from?

'Head—neck…' Then she closed her eyes.

'Sherazad!' The frenzied shout ripped out of him. Emilio gave him a rough shake.

'Snap out of it, Lorenzo. Either you take care of her, or move aside and let me do it. Daniel is more qualified than you in dealing with a head and neck injury. His truck will soon catch up with us.'

Someone else taking care of her? No! The idea had him focused in a heartbeat.

He had her exposed in seconds and a lightning examination confirmed her own diagnosis. His tears ran faster. 'Why do you always have to be right…?'

He stifled his sobbing. It was the last thing she needed to hear. If she could hear. He had to hang onto the positive part. It seemed she'd turned away at the last second, escaping a total frontal injury. Her face and her vital organs had escaped unscathed, but the shrapnel had showered her right side, riddling it with a multitude of superficial wounds. Her scalp wounds were bleeding extensively. But the real injury, the one that had him going numb and nauseous with fear, was her neck injury. She was showing all the 'hard' signs of serious vascular injury. Severe pulsing bleeding, shock unresponsive to fluid administration, diminished consciousness and pulses away from the site of injury.

He bit down hard on his lower lip, drawing blood, steadying himself, keeping the direct pressure applied to her head and neck wounds. 'Emilio, set up the mobile theatre. I must operate now.'

'Shall I prepare X-ray for angiography?' Emilio asked anxiously.

'No need. This is a zone two injury and examination is enough to tell me its extent. Pass me a Foley's catheter before you go. And prepare ten units of A-positive blood, if we have it, and six units plasma and platelets.'

Emilio bolted to do his bidding, and he turned his attention to stemming Sherazad's bleeding. He guided the catheter into the injury tract. Once he'd passed it inside the artery spurting blood, he inflated it, closing the injury as much as possible. He talked to her constantly as he reassessed her status. 'Sherazad, *mia amore*, talk to me, *tesoro…*'

She murmured incoherently behind the mask, opened unseeing eyes, then closed them again. Another salvo of desperation detonated in his gut. With her carotid artery injury she could have a stroke!

He shouted for help and both Gulnar and Derek straightened from Ashjay's side and rushed over to him. Ben scooped the boy off the ground. He met their eyes, one by one.

Ashjay was gone.

'*No!* The monsters! The inhuman filth…' His ranting stuck in his throat. He couldn't afford pain and fury. He had to focus everything he had, everything he was, on saving Sherazad. He forced out his directions in choking words. 'Apply direct pressure to the venous and scalp bleeding while I do a neurological exam.'

Two minutes later, feeling blackness descending on him, he breathed again. At least he'd found no neurological signs of stroke or brain damage.

In minutes they'd transferred her to the mobile theatre unit—a van attached to one of their trucks, with its own air-conditioning system, a complete operating room and a two-patient intensive care unit.

They scrubbed in record time and prepped Sherazad. The moment Ben had her under, Lorenzo reported her injuries, his lips warping around the horrifying words. 'We have an internal jugular vein and external carotid artery injury, plus scalp and flesh wounds on right arm, torso, thigh and leg. I'll take care of vascular repair, while you handle the rest. *Prego Dio*, all other vital structures of the neck seem intact, but I'll—I'll have to explore to make sure.'

He knew Daniel was out there, ready to take over at a second's notice if it got too much for him. He looked at her. Intubated, fragile and whiter than the sheet she lay on. He looked at the mangled neck he'd tasted and buried all his hunger and passion in.

It *was* too much. His love and fear were nearly driving him to his knees. But he had to do this, had to be the one who fought for her life.

It was reassuring, knowing someone he trusted could step in if he crumpled. But he wouldn't.

Sherazad's eyes scratched open. Every inch of her body sent distress signals of pain and numbness. She'd been in and out of…sedation? For how long? Hours? Days? More? She didn't care. As long as Lorenzo was there.

And he was there, keeping vigil by her bed.

She reached out to him. Her hand snagged on an IV line. He instantly came to her, enfolding her hand and getting down on his knees beside her bed. She tried to drag him up to her, to feel his lips and body on hers. He came up, but only his lips touched her forehead.

His days' old beard scratched her, its silver streaks already formed. His eyes were muddy in their reddish haze. He looked unkempt and pale and spent—and the most magnificent thing she'd ever seen.

Love burst inside her. 'Kiss me, Lorenzo.' Her voice was thick and rough, sandpaper lining her larynx. Had she been intubated? What had happened? Somehow, she wasn't worried. Lorenzo was here. It was all that mattered.

'You're almost back to normal if you're thinking of kissing already.'

'Not any kissing—*our* kissing!' She tugged him again. But this time he didn't even come closer. She sighed. 'Can you get me my backpack?'

No snappy comeback was thrown her way as usual. He just blinked and went blank. He had to be beyond exhaustion.

'For a toothbrush and toothpaste? So I can get that kiss?' She could barely move her lips, but she smiled all her tenderness and longing.

His smile looked forced as he sat back down in his chair, almost falling the last part of the way.

Concern kicked in her heart. 'You look…finished.'

He covered his face with both hands and gave a derisive huff of laughter. 'Thanks.'

'You can look both terrific and tired, darling. So why don't you go and rest? Better still, come here and rest? I promise, I'm in no shape for anything but deep cuddling.'

'You rest, Sherazad. This chair has been my bed for the last three days.'

'So I wasn't imagining it! You *have* been sitting beside me all that time. But what about work? Who's taking care of everything?'

'It's all going according to schedule. After the accident…' He stopped and suddenly everything came back to her with a force that made her cry out.

Lorenzo shot to his feet. 'Where do you hurt? Is it your neck? Where?'

Her neck… She touched a tentative hand to the heavy

bandage there, her mind deluged by flashes of slicing pain, suffocating dread, a mind-blowing boom—and Ashjay…

'Ashjay?'

She read the truth in his bleak eyes.

Horror caught in her throat, and his arms finally came around her. She sank into his comfort and sobbed herself into oblivion again.

Consciousness returned to the feel of him all around her, filling her with solace and peace.

She slowly pieced together what had happened. The only thing she didn't know was how badly she'd been injured and how hard he'd fought for her life. She could move everything, so she knew her nervous system was intact. But she remembered the second her neck had been slashed, remembered feeling her life drain away with every heartbeat.

'Lorenzo…' He stirred immediately and got off the bed. She tried to cling to him, but her fingers were dough and he slipped through them. What was wrong? Why didn't he want to stay near her? A debilitating suspicion hit her, hard. 'How bad do I look?'

His reassurance was hasty, but he sounded and looked…weird. Expressionless. 'Your face is untouched. As for the rest of your injuries, we employed the best aesthetic techniques in suturing them, so you should have negligible scarring. You don't have a scarring tendency anyway. I had to borrow a piece of the great saphenous vein in your foot to patch your carotid artery and we had to cut your hair very short to stitch your scalp.'

'I was thinking of cutting it anyway.' She just had to interrupt this clinical report. What was wrong with him? Why was he avoiding looking her in the eye? Was he telling her something?

She tried to get up, to escape her oppressive thoughts. His powerful hands stopped her. The hands that had snatched her from death's jaws. That had sent her to heaven. That now touched her with nothing but the detached concern of a surgeon and a compassionate stranger. She couldn't bear it. 'I need to move...'

He was gentle yet adamant as he eased her back down. 'As soon as your temperature's down and you start eating. You must be a mass of soreness. I'll top off your pain relief and you can go back to sleep.'

Every injury was a searing brand. Yet that wasn't why she welcomed the relief of senselessness again. The physical pain would have been endurable if it hadn't been combined with the emotional pain of Ashjay's death—and of Lorenzo's withdrawal.

Lorenzo was dedicated to her.

But only in his medical capacity.

At first Sherazad tried to tell herself he wasn't as demonstrative as usual on account of her injuries. Then the days passed, and she felt better, and he allowed her transfer from the ward to a room.

Her room, not theirs. His withdrawal was real and complete. He no longer wanted her.

She'd dreaded the day he'd stop wanting her, wondered how it would happen, how he would behave, how it would feel.

It had happened—just like that. He behaved like her concerned surgeon. It felt worse than having her neck slashed.

She couldn't understand it. If it had been only sex for him, how could she have lost her appeal so suddenly, so totally? Could it have anything to do with him operating on her? Had it somehow put him off?

Three weeks after her surgery, she gave in. She had to beg him—for anything. She had to have...something. At best, a rekindling. At worst, closure.

What she got was the final twist of the dagger in her heart.

She stood at his door, heard him moving inside. She gathered all her courage and knocked. He didn't answer. She swallowed her agitation and called to him. 'Lorenzo...?'

A moment of silence followed then he called out, 'You're late again, Gulnar. Come in already, *mia amore*!'

'Traitor!'

Sherazad turned calmly at the accusation. She stood by the army truck that would take her to Montenegro International Airport, and watched the colleagues who'd come to mean so much to her getting ready to say goodbye.

Lorenzo was not with them.

'Deserter.' Derek gave her a good-natured wink. 'Leaving us in the lurch overhauling this fossilised medical facility!'

'A landmine blowing up in your face has a way of changing your mind, *amigo*.' Emilio handed her a lovely handmade local scarf, with her name entwined ingeniously into the pattern.

She cried out her pleasure and hugged him. 'Emilio, that's so thoughtful, so precious. I'll treasure it.'

Derek handed her his souvenir, an oil landscape by a local artist of a neighbouring area she'd admired. 'I had bets you'd stay longer than your six months. Do you have any idea how much I'm losing?'

Ben hugged her and slipped a silver locket on a chain over her head. 'If you'd stayed, I'd be the one to lose a tidy sum. Not that I'd mind.'

So Ben had predicted the end. They probably all had. Only Derek, with his enduring naïvety, had miscalculated. Like her.

Gulnar was the last. She gave Sherazad three books then hauled her, books and all, into a fierce hug. 'The translated version isn't as powerful as the original. But they'll tell you how things really are in this part of the world.'

Sherazad wondered at her lack of animosity. This was the woman who'd replaced her in Lorenzo's passion. But what she felt towards Gulnar wasn't hatred or even jealousy. It was overwhelming sadness. For Gulnar's misguided self-preservation, for Emilio's heartache. But mostly for

Lorenzo's fickleness. It was beneath the great man that he was…

But how dared she call him fickle? His vocation was far greater than any personal involvement. He had to have comfort wherever it was offered to keep on functioning at top efficiency, making a difference in the world. And he'd never promised her anything, had warned her from the beginning how it would be.

In a few minutes, goodbyes and exchanges of addresses and email addresses were concluded and they'd transferred her limited belongings to the truck.

Then she felt him. Coming to say goodbye.

She had to restrain herself from jumping into the truck and begging her peace-keeping escorts to drive out of there at top speed. She'd been avoiding him ever since that day outside his door. Not that she'd had to. He'd avoided her just as much. She knew it was over, had never been real, but she still didn't want to see it written all over him.

It was too late. He was there, so close she could feel his heat, his spirit.

The last thing she'd see of him, the memory that would replace her joyous memories of him, the one she'd carry with her in the desolate years to come, would be of his eyes emptied of intimacy and caring.

'Sherazad…'

Her eyes squeezed shut. She'd never hear his voice again. Never have her senses stir and soar again. She'd shared more than her body with him. She'd shared her all! How could she live without the happiness, the security of being understood and appreciated? How could she live, knowing it would never be repeated?

How could he just forget her like that? Replace her like that?

Oh, God, why couldn't he have felt the same? If not for ever then at least for longer…?

She squashed the pathetic thoughts, struggled with the sick electricity arcing in her flesh. She'd promised herself never to be another man's victim, and she was letting Lorenzo make her a worse victim than Jack ever had. With Jack, her heart and soul had never been breached, just her self-confidence and dignity. Lorenzo's damage was total.

But she was honest enough to admit it was her doing, not his. Fair enough to acknowledge she still owed him for freeing her from her bitternesses and insecurities. She'd pay her dues.

'Lorenzo!' She turned to face him, intercepting any uneasy words, promising anything if only her lips didn't tremble, if her eyes didn't fill. 'I would have written if I'd left without seeing you. I wanted to thank you for all the good you do. It's been a privilege and an honour being a part of your team. This has been the most incredible experience of my life. A non-stop adventure of epic proportions. I doubt anything will ever touch it.'

His eyes were blank. It was worse than she'd expected, this emptiness. Was he doing it on purpose? What was he thinking? Was he pitying her, babbling like this? Was he feeling sorry he'd got involved with her at all? Was it too awkward, having to face her this last time? Did he have to look so beautiful, so precious, so unforgettable?

'I'm glad you enjoyed yourself.' His voice was neutral, then suddenly he groaned. 'I didn't mean it that way! I'm—'

'It's all right!' She cut him short again. She wouldn't survive it if he said he was sorry. 'I *did* enjoy myself. Our relationship was the most timely, liberating thing that could have happened to me. Thanks to you, I'm whole again—ready to live and love once more.'

'Dr Dawson,' her escort prompted. 'If you're ready?'

She grabbed the interruption like a lifeline. 'Yes, yes, I am.' She turned to Lorenzo, found his golden eyes ablaze, his jaw and his fists clenched. So he *had* been projecting indifference. He did feel bad...

She couldn't help it. Her arms went around his waist, her head pressed over his heart and, for one last time, she basked in his nearness, made believe he cared.

This would be her last memory of him.

'Goodbye, Lorenzo. Maybe in another life.'

Lorenzo felt as if his life was slipping away as her truck receded into the distance.

Instead of feeling grateful that she was leaving and with such a positive outlook he was enraged and agonised. Hearing her say she'd start her life over, without him, loving someone else, was eroding his sanity, sapping his will to live. He couldn't envision life without her, felt like killing any man she might think of having a relationship with.

He wanted her back immediately—and for ever. And she would have stayed if he'd only asked.

But how could he have asked? She'd almost died in his arms!

He still woke up suffocating, his pillow drenched, remembering the horror and desperation of feeling her life slipping through his fingers, reliving the hours he'd fought to hang onto her. If they hadn't had immediate operating facilities she would have died. At best, she would have been crippled. If she stayed, she'd still be in constant danger. Next time she might not be so lucky.

There was really no choice.

No matter how vital to his life and sanity she was, or that he'd never know another moment of peace or happiness without her, he couldn't risk her life. Ever again.

And he couldn't go after her and back into the world. He hadn't lived a normal life in so long he knew he couldn't live one again. Even if he could, how could he relinquish the pledge he'd made at Piero's deathbed?

Her truck was no longer visible on the green horizon of the clear May day. The weather was balmy and fragrant, their work was coming together. Things in general were starting to look up for the region in conflict.

Inside him, there was only devastation.

His world had touched Sherazad's for a brief, life-

changing time. Now she was going back where she belonged.

He'd remain here, where he had to be, alone.

Without her, he'd be alone anywhere, for ever.

CHAPTER ELEVEN

'I'M NOT asking! I *demand*...' Sherazad paused, lowered her voice with a great effort then continued, 'to return to the Sredna refugee camp.'

It was safe to return. Lorenzo was taking another mission, away from the Balkans. So she wanted to return to the place where she'd felt most useful, most needed. But they were denying her request.

The GAO political liaison eyed her with complete detachment, then rose, clearly ending the interview. 'I'm sorry, Dr Dawson,' he said in that aggravating nasal tone. 'The decision came from higher up.'

'But why?' she cried. 'I won't believe the camp doesn't still need doctors. Or is it just me you don't want? I thought my record with you was exemplary!'

'It is. And if you're anxious to go on a field mission, I've been authorised to offer you one in Ethiopia—'

'I don't *want* to go to Ethiopia; I want to return to the Balkans!'

'Not possible. And until those responsible for mission deployment decide otherwise, you'd better accept that. Good day, Dr Dawson.'

Minutes later, huffing in the sticky late August afternoon, she slammed into her car and joined central London's heavy traffic.

Good day, he'd said! It couldn't be a worse day.

Her days were in a steady decline from miserable to dismal.

It had been three months since she'd come home. She'd immediately sought to submerge herself in work. Luckily, GAO had snapped her up, offering her a surgical training post in one of their affiliated hospitals, and an aid operation co-ordinator's position in their central office.

To her family and to the outside world, it seemed she'd come back from the frontline focused, productive, with a new purpose in life and unlimited drive. Inside she felt nothing but a monumental sense of let-down and futility.

She was doing a good job—a great one, according to her superiors and colleagues—her professional confidence and performance of the highest standard. But any medical work seemed tame and uninteresting in comparison with the immediacy of frontline practice. Being a long-distance aid worker was nowhere near as satisfying as reaching people herself in their most acute need.

And every day she woke up to life without Lorenzo, every time she needed to turn to him for support, counsel, validation or passion, knowing he wasn't there, she died. Then had to live again, when she didn't want to.

She groped for solace from her mother, who told her time would heal her. But time only deepened her wounds.

Then she reached a point where she rebelled against her pathetic feelings. She forcibly reminded herself she'd sworn to never let another man make her miserable. She wasn't letting anyone else control her well-being, in any way, ever again.

So she stopped following Lorenzo's news and moves. And when her mother advised her to let other men into her life, her answer was an emphatic, 'No way!' She didn't need a man, or anyone or anything else for that matter, to complete her, to make her life worthwhile.

So why was she thinking her days were dismal?

So what if she was having a difficult time professionally and taking time out personally? She'd come a long way, and she should be proud of what she'd accomplished!

Screeching to a halt in her apartment building's car park, she grabbed her bag and sprinted inside. She'd bathe, then rush to GAO's office building and accomplish some more. She'd give whoever was responsible for that stupid ban that had been placed on her an earful. She was going back to the frontline.

Fifteen minutes later, she was just about to wash her hair when her doorbell rang. Again and again.

She heaved herself out of the bubbles and ran, dripping, to her bedroom. She dried herself haphazardly and jumped into the first things her hands reached in her closet. The doorbell rang again, and she stormed to the door.

Her next-door neighbour was at it again, inventing any excuse to ring her bell and strike up a conversation. And she'd had it with him and his inability to get her polite messages of 'thanks but, no, thanks'. She'd bet he wouldn't be so eager after she'd yelled him back to his apartment. She wasn't cultivating another Jack!

She snatched the door open and her berating words died on her lips.

For there, standing tall and broad and indescribable, was Lorenzo.

Lorenzo.

It couldn't be.

He was somewhere on some frontline. No matter what she told herself, she was just so starved for him she was still imagining that she saw him everywhere.

But this time the illusion didn't fade, didn't metamorphose into another man.

He was really there.

Everything in her surged. In jubilation. In confusion.

Then everything ceased to exist. He closed the gap between them, his eager smile everything that had kept her awake night after night.

'Sherazad, *amore!*' He hugged her off the floor and she nearly fainted with the pressure of emotions and sensations.

Lorenzo, oh, my love! I've withered without you.

A couple of her neighbours passed by, openly curious. But she was beyond caring. Lorenzo was here, holding her again… But why?

Her mind tried to kickstart, to make sense of it all. Why

was he here in London—between missions? Looking her up since he was already around, since he now considered her a fond acquaintance? Or, worse, was he after some more no-strings fun while he tended to the matters he really cared about?

Well, whatever his motives for being there, she wasn't doing this. She had decided to forget him. It was over!

It was still the most difficult thing she'd had to do, pushing herself out of his arms. His hands clung to her, trying to keep her close, so she took one more step back, taking herself out of his reach. If he didn't touch her, she'd pull it off, stand her ground.

'What are you doing here?' She hoped she sounded as remote as she wanted to be.

The eagerness in his eyes faltered, to be replaced by a more dangerous emotion. Something hot and hungry. Strike the 'fond acquaintance' theory! 'I'm here to see you, hopefully to take you out.'

It was then she noticed the suit. The first dressy thing she'd seen on him. And the way that immaculate slate-grey contained his elemental power—and that trim haircut… He simply hurt her with his beauty!

But take her out? Just like that? After he'd cut her off, then left her without as much as a word for three months, he expected to walk back into her life and whisk her away? Of all the nerve…

But even fury didn't make her strong enough to withstand his devouring gaze head on. She focused her gaze between his Adam's apple and his tie, and prayed for enough steadiness to deliver the snub. 'I'm sorry you came for nothing, then. I have a full day tomorrow and I was planning an early night.'

'Oh?' He pursed his lips and leaned on the doorframe. 'You sleep in…this?' His eyes swept her clingy burgundy stretch top and trousers, a tight smile twisting his lips, a leap of masculine ferocity entering his eyes. 'Or are you expecting someone to share your early night?'

What? What did he care? How dared he ask? Did he think he had a claim on her still? Was he presuming to be jealous?

Suddenly whatever remained of the sheer shock and pleasure of having him near again disappeared. 'And what business is it of yours?'

'Apparently none.' There was that feral smile again, the velvet barely hiding the spikes of anger. 'So you have another lover already? You weren't kidding, then, when you said you were ready to live and love again!'

That was rich! Her blood boiled. '*Already?* You make it sound as if it's been three days, instead of three months.' He'd let her go without a word. He'd taken another lover even before she'd left. How dared he talk as if he felt betrayed? 'I am free to take another lover—*any* number of lovers—whenever I want to! I'm also sure you know what you can do with your double standard, Dr Chauvinist.'

She held his incensed gaze with an even fiercer one of her own. It was his that relented, the flame extinguished. 'Duly reprimanded, *tesoro.*'

Oh, no! He wasn't playing the irresistible, innocent devil with her again. 'Listen, Lorenzo. This is really a bad idea. If only you'd called, you would have saved yourself the drive. And I was actually going out, grabbing the last working hours in GAO Central to file a complaint. So if you'll excuse me...'

He held up his hands, his smile plastered back on, looking totally unconvincing this time. 'Fine. So you have other plans. Only fair. But I see you're not ready yet. How about you invite me in while you dress and we can talk for a while? Maybe I can drive you there?'

Before she could say that she was finished with inviting heartache and misery into her life, he straightened and gently pushed past her into her apartment.

Once in the middle of her cosy reception area, he exhaled, raked his incredible hair with his fingers, making a visible effort to relax his taut features. Then he looked around and his smile turned genuine. 'It's all you. Unique colours and an overall spellbinding effect.'

His deep, intimate whisper thrilled through her. She barely curbed her shuddering response. How many times had she imagined seeing him here? Reality was far better.

But she was too angry at his presumption, at—everything, to savour the poignancy of his presence in her home, the pleasure of his praise.

'Aren't you getting dressed?' he finally asked when she stood there staring at him, not knowing what to blurt out first. 'Shall *I* get undressed?'

That unlocked her paralysed speech centres. 'So you *do* think you can just pick up where you left off!'

He prowled to where she stood, baring his fierce desire to her, snatching hers from her depths, starting a molten churning in her core. 'I don't think. I pray. I know I'm not entitled to anything, but I still pray for everything.' He caught her in mighty, trembling arms, pressed her to his need and buried his face in her now healed neck. '*Ti amo, mia amore*. I've left the frontline—to come to you—if you'll have me.'

This was her fantasy! Her impossible dream! She'd wake up any moment now, alone and cold and empty. For ever.

But Lorenzo was still here, his ragged words of love filling her awareness, his hard body rocking against her, turning hers to liquid lust.

She had a million questions. He answered one.

'I couldn't come to you before Brezny's hospital became operational and reasonably modernised. Before I came to terms with things, and arranged everything else. It's been three months in hell.' His arms convulsed around her, his body deepening the intimacy of their embrace.

Lorenzo loved her. Needed her. He'd given up his vocation to be with her. It was heaven. It was completely unexpected. Inconceivable.

Shocking.

Her elation ebbed.

What if he was just passing through a phase of mental and physical exhaustion, and thought he couldn't go on any more? Thought she'd be his haven while he recharged himself? She'd never survive another parting from him.

She had an even bigger fear. What if he *had* given it all up for her? It would be such a great sacrifice for him. What if she wasn't enough to replace the excitement, the achievement and the variety of women he was used to?

But her greatest fear was his disturbing, unknown intensity. It brought back all her fears of placing herself in another man's emotional focus. She'd felt safe loving him, because his emotional distance and control had been an integral part of his character. What if he turned into another obsessive lover? What if it was she who brought out the irrational, the violent in men?

Her heart pleaded for him, for anything at all with him, for any length of time, under any conditions.

Self-preservation won.

She pushed out of his embrace on quivering legs. He followed her, devoured her. She came up from his kiss gasping, fear blinding her. 'I hope you haven't made any permanent plans on my account. I don't want to take up where we left off. Once was enough.'

Sherazad's whispered words deafened Lorenzo, stopped his heart.

She couldn't mean them. She couldn't have fallen out of love with him this fast. But…what if she had fallen in love with someone else?

The thought of another man's lips on hers, his body entwined with hers… Jealousy scorched his mind, leaving insanity in its wake. 'Why? Because you've really moved on? There really is another man? Answer me!'

He watched her ebony eyes widening with shock, then horror. 'What if I have? What if there is? What would you do? Hit me?'

Her accusation jolted him. She thought it a possibility he might lash out at her? Resort to violence to settle the dispute, to vent his frustration? Like Jack? No wonder she was frantically pushing him away. But he had to admit he *was* giving her every reason to fear him, behaving like that.

He drew in a long, steadying breath. He had to be supremely careful if he wasn't to alienate her for ever. 'Hit you? *Dio*, Sherazad—where did that come from? How can you even think it? So I'm being a jealous fool, but you know I'd never, *ever* hurt you.'

He watched her closely. Her whole body relaxed gradually, her eyes losing that desperate look. But fear was gone only to be replaced by wariness.

'Sherazad, for God's sake, tell me you know I'd rather die than hurt you.'

Her eyes darted away from his face, and she nodded, looking almost embarrassed. 'I know.'

So why was she still so afraid? Did she fear his love? Did she think he'd suffocate her with it? Again, like Jack?

He approached her and she tensed. His heart bled at the loss of her trust. He couldn't live without it. Had to do anything to restore it. He had to downplay his need, his dependence. He had to convince her he hadn't changed the course of his life for her. It wasn't fair to burden her with that sort of emotional debt. At least until she realised it had been no sacrifice. He also had to stress her total freedom— her emotional, personal and every other sort of freedom. Now and for ever.

He drew her into a loose embrace and this time she stood there, looking up at him, soft and unique, his every hope and dream come to life. He traced the faint scars on her neck and she shuddered.

'Did you know I just turned forty? I've always heard the milestone makes a man take stock of his life, and it turned out to be true. Then I lost another co-worker on the frontline…' She gasped and he soothed her. 'No one you know. Someone *I* barely knew, but it didn't hit me any less. This time it told me I've had enough. So here I am. Taking my pledge to Piero to another battlefield, maybe less immediate, far less dangerous, but still as important, maybe even helping far more people in need. I've taken up the administrative chief of operations position in GAO Central. And if you want, if you're free, I do want to pick up where we left off, one wonderful, ecstatic day at a time…'

He bent his head and traced her scars with his tongue and she jerked and moaned. She wanted him still, thank God. She still looked confused, but he wouldn't give worries a chance to prey on her mind.

He slipped one hand beneath her stretch top and the other into her trousers, gliding his roughened hands over her satiny flesh, cupping one perfect hip and breast, teasing her tight nipple and sliding in and out of the valley between her buttocks. She cried out his name. He drank it in and fed her his tongue. Her taste surged to his head and his loins. He'd starved for her. *Starved!* He needed her hard and fast. But how did she need him?

With a wild whimper, she sucked his tongue, ground her breasts into him, pulled him down to her with all her strength, a trembling leg around his hips.

She needed hard and fast too!

In minutes, she was writhing on their scattered clothes on the floor, with him on top of her, inside her, pounding away at her clinging, greedy flesh, her frenzied cries of pleasure discharging explosions in his blood, transporting him to an unknown level of ecstasy.

Her cries became a keening scream as she suddenly bucked and froze, then shattered around him, wrenching his own climactic release from him, milking him of every last drop of passion.

He collapsed on top of her, shuddering with the unbearable happiness of coming home inside her. He crushed her beneath him, just like she'd always asked him to, begging for his weight on her in the aftermath of ecstasy, lest she just dissolve in satisfaction.

He had her again.

Everything was going to be perfect.

*   *   *

Sherazad surfaced from the delirium. She hugged him to her, inside her, and warded off the malignant thoughts.

They wouldn't be kept at bay.

She didn't want him to give up his vocation on her account, for every reason there was. But when he'd told her he hadn't, it had crushed her nevertheless. She'd jumped to stupid conclusions again. Not only wouldn't Lorenzo turn obsessive, he probably wouldn't be committed—or monogamous.

Her heart and body thought having him one wonderful, ecstatic day at a time was enough. They told her she was being ridiculous and contradictory. Hadn't the thought of his fierce involvement scared her witless?

But it was like something had fallen into place inside her. She no longer feared the intensity of his emotions. Now she needed a commitment, and she loved him too much to start again without one.

She *wanted* him demanding and possessive. She knew beyond a doubt that he'd never be morbid with it. If she were his, if he had her vows and her future happiness in his hands, he would cherish, not strangle, her, enrich her life, not destroy it. She knew the depth of passion and commitment he was capable of. But she had to face it. She wasn't the one to inspire them in him. And she wasn't sticking around to witness the day he found the woman who would.

She loosened her hold on him, and he rose above her, melting her with his smile of passion and indulgence. Then he bent to her again, drowning her in soul-stealing kisses, hardening fully inside her, starting their love-making all over again.

If she took him again, she'd take him for ever.

But he wasn't offering for ever. Just until it ended again.

She squirmed beneath him and he stopped immediately and withdrew, completely this time. The last time.

Aching and trembling with the loss of his body from hers,

she scrambled to her knees. His eyes bored into her, intense, uncertain, making it even harder to regain her co-ordination.

She rushed to her bedroom for clothes that didn't bear the mark of their passion. He followed her, stopping her as she clasped her bra.

'What is it, *amore*?' He pulled her back against his hard body, anxiety and solicitude vibrating in his voice, his hands roaming over her in soothing motions that only maddened her with longing. 'What did I do?'

Lorenzo's heart thudded as she bolted away from him again, putting the width of the bed between them.

'Everything perfectly.' She put on her clothes, her voice ragged. 'I couldn't have asked for better closure.'

The word fell on him like a wrecking ball. 'Closure?'

'We never had a proper goodbye.' She attempted a chuckle. It came out weak and artificial.

'And this was…it?'

'Yes.'

He stared at her as she finished dressing then pushed past him, leaving him standing there paralysed in the middle of her bedroom.

So this was it. There was no escaping the crippling truth.

He'd tried the truth about his feelings and had only managed to scare her. He'd tried the watered-down fiction and had only made it easy for her to end it once and for all. It was time he admitted it. He'd been living a fiction.

He'd misread everything she'd said and done back on the frontline. He'd seen and heard what he'd wanted to. He'd thought she'd been hoping for a continuation with him, when she'd probably been only hoping for a prolongation of the adventure of sexual healing and freedom from inhibitions.

That was all he'd been to her. An adventure.

An adventure that had come to an end.

All the love, the uniqueness, all the dreams of a future; the ones she'd been horrified about when he'd revealed them, had been on his side.

If he pursued her now, he'd be no better than Jack...
But...no!

He was *nothing* like Jack. And she should know. She did
know. His love for her was healthy and pure and he had to
offer it to her, offer her all the happiness and fulfilment it
could bring her—had once brought her. He couldn't give
up.

He wouldn't be so afraid he'd remind her of Jack that
he'd go to the other extreme and let her end it without a
fight.

It was time he told her how it was going to be, that he'd
remain around her, for ever if need be, until he regained her
trust and earned her love. What else had he to live for, if
not the hope of recapturing what they'd had?

He walked out of her bedroom and followed her subdued
voice to where she sat talking on the phone in her living
room. '...mission in Ethiopia. When can I come to sign on?'

She listened for a moment before saying, 'Very well.'
Then she hung up. She turned to him. 'Still here? I meant
it about this being goodbye, Lorenzo.'

He ignored the pang her cold words and aloof expression
caused him, and almost sighed with relief. She'd just taken
one of his auxiliary plans. 'If you're going to Ethiopia, it
will be at least a year until we say goodbye.'

That got a reaction from her. A spectacular one. 'You
mean *you're* going? But—but you—you said you're taking
the chief of operations position...' Her stammering stopped,
incredulity flashing across her delightful face, followed by
anger—no, fury! 'It was you, wasn't it? You're the one who
banned me from returning to the Balkans!'

Sherazad watched him nod his wary admission. And well
might he be wary. She felt like taking a swing at him. How
dared he manipulate her like that?

She snatched the handset up again. 'I'm cancelling my
appointment. I'm damned if I let you herd me into whatever
slot you have vacant!'

He stopped her, his face stern, his voice deep and serious.

'You *know* this operation needs you more. The people there have been suffering far longer.'

He was right, of course. Her personal anger deflated on a wave of shame. She'd wanted the mission for her own ends again, so she could bury her personal misery in the chaos all around her.

She let the handset clang to its cradle and sagged back on the couch. He came down to sit beside her. He was only in his trousers, and the sight of his chest, the memory of her lips and teeth there... She snatched her gaze away, pressing down hard on the debilitating yearning.

'But you have the right idea about leaving,' he said, his words slow and careful. 'I doubt whether I can work in an office and a regular hospital again either. I thought I'd give it a try, but I made it clear I'd only be available if...' He stopped.

If what? she nearly cried out. If she stayed around and took up his offer of an affair? *Did* she have anything to do with his decision-making? Or had he only been allowing for the probability that a day behind a desk would send him running to the field again?

He interrupted her chaotic thoughts, his tone still deliberate. 'Anyway, there are two other candidates for the position, so I'm free to go at any time. And as it was me who arranged the Ethiopian mission, I know we can be there within the week.'

'And you'll be head of my mission again!' She said it out loud, as if hearing it would help her come to terms with the implications.

Lorenzo, wanting her again, near again, every minute of every day, working together, depending on each other... How could she resist him?

She exhaled angrily. She'd gone on without him, hadn't she? And she'd still do so now. Tonight, he'd just taken her by surprise, and...

And who was she kidding? She'd gone on without him only because she'd had no choice. If he'd walked out today, taken no for an answer, he would have again taken the choice from her hands. But he hadn't walked out, and he would stay near, making the choice hers again. Did she think for a moment she could resist her love for him?

She raised her eyes to him and she could swear he was following her inner turmoil, something invading his golden eyes: challenge? Determination? And was that a touch of entreaty too? Whatever it was, it slammed her heart against her ribs.

At last he spoke, low and husky, 'You have a problem with that?'

'Not unless you intend to create one.' She tried to sound nonchalant. And failed. It was no use. She would succumb.

But she'd had many revelations in the last hour. She'd gone from her original denial to anger to fear to acceptance. She now knew she'd take the time she could with him. But this time she'd go in with her eyes open. She'd take responsibility for her own actions and expectations. This way, nothing that he did, nothing that would happen, would ever hurt her again.

Lorenzo kept trying to follow the dizzying succession of emotions on her face. She was still irritated. But there were so many other things! Resignation? Yielding? He prayed so. Whatever she was feeling, he had to put his cards on the table. 'You'll create it if you expect to work together and not be lovers again. You might as well give in now and let's go to bed. I want you again—and again.'

He really could have said that better! But it was out and he braced himself for a barrage of fury at his high-handed confidence when he had none, thrashing about in blind desperation. Instead, she gave him such a solemn look…

Dio! He'd just burnt all his bridges—of all the stupid things to say!

Then she opened her mouth and turned his world upside down.

Had she just said, 'All right!'?

Then she turned him inside out again, going on, her voice fracturing. 'But I ask for a commitment first.'

What? His self-sufficient Sherazad? He'd never even dared… 'Are you proposing to me, *amore*?' The words were out before he could stop them. He was on a self-destruct mission every time he opened his mouth!

Her whole body in the sleeveless cream dress blushed, just like when he overloaded her senses with pleasure. He shifted with the expanding heaviness of arousal, even as he waited with a thundering heart for her to end his hopes.

Her 'No, no!' was flustered, and he thought, *There!* Proof he'd misunderstood her again—that he was the most pathetic man on earth.

But she went on, 'I just need a declaration of your intentions. If we become lovers again, I intend to love you, cherish every moment with you, for better or for worse for as long as you want me. In return I only ask for total honesty when you want it to end, or when you want to be with someone else. If you can't promise monogamy while you're with me, then forget it.'

He stared at her precious beauty, his blood roaring in his head, his heart expanding with agonising suddenness, filling his whole body.

She loved him.

Sherazad *loved* him.

So much she'd bestow her love on him even if he didn't love her back. It was more than he deserved, more than anyone deserved. Humble tears rushed to his eyes and he had her on his lap in one hungry move.

He buried his ragged relief in her neck. 'You tormentress! What I promise is glorious retribution. Were you torturing me for letting you walk out of Badovna?'

She pushed his head away so she could glare her reproach at him. 'It's the least you deserve. In fact, whatever you say to rationalise what you did to me, if you're foolish enough to place yourself in my power, be duly warned that I'm not finished torturing you back.'

He laughed. Though he wasn't sure if he should. Her words were teasing but her eyes… He was still on precarious ground. She might love him, but she'd lost her faith in him.

He had to have it back. 'You can do anything at all to me, as long as you love me. But don't you understand why I did what I did? I had to make you go. When I thought I was losing you—I wouldn't wish that kind of terror and desperation on my worst enemy. I couldn't let you endanger yourself again. I *won't*. That's why I changed your mission options. I came here, keeping my options open, until I knew where you wanted to be. It's all the same to me as long as I'm with you, doing what we do best, saving lives.'

She closed her eyes on a deep, tremulous inhalation, as if she hadn't been breathing till just now. Then she opened them and it squeezed his heart to see the lingering pain in their wetness. 'And…Gulnar?'

Would she believe him? 'Do you really think I didn't know it was you outside my door that night? I only used her as your repellent, as she was using me as Emilio's.'

Her eyes cleared, and he could see it—instant belief. His sweet, strong, selfless Sherazad needed only his word to believe him, and in him.

Her smile held all the love and trust he'd been unable to live without. It wrapped around his heart, lit up his soul. She made him feel the only man on earth, with all the urgency, heat and tenderness of her uninhibited passion.

Before he lost his mind completely, he had to make sure she was totally secure in his love. He grasped her hands and brought her face up to his. 'I can pledge my love, but I'll let time show you. Fifty years from now you'll believe that I can never want, or be with, anyone else. I've been yours since the moment you shot me. You struck me down for good.'

Her eyes shone with love and tears. Then she freed her hands and resumed driving him insane. 'And you retaliated, remember? Knocked me down, got me right there and then.

But with this Sherazad you're getting far more than a thousand and one nights. Say ten thousand and one?'

He fell silent, busy calculating. Then he exclaimed, 'Every *other* night for the next fifty years? You *do* plan to torture me, don't you?'

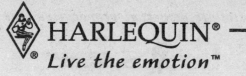

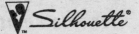

Silhouette®

SILHOUETTE Romance®

From first love to forever, these love stories
are fairy tale romances for today's woman.

Silhouette® Desire®

Modern, passionate reads that are powerful and provocative.

Silhouette® SPECIAL EDITION™

Emotional, compelling stories that capture the intensity
of living, loving and creating a family in today's world.

Silhouette® INTIMATE MOMENTS™

A roller-coaster read that delivers romantic thrills
in a world of suspense, adventure and more.

 Harlequin Historicals®
Historical Romantic Adventure!

*From rugged lawmen and
valiant knights to defiant heiresses
and spirited frontierswomen,
Harlequin Historicals will
capture your imagination with
their dramatic scope, passion
and adventure.*

*Harlequin Historicals . . .
they're too good to miss!*

HARLEQUIN®
INTRIGUE®

WE'LL LEAVE YOU BREATHLESS!

If you've been looking for thrilling tales of contemporary passion and sensuous love stories with taut, edge-of-the-seat suspense—then you'll love Harlequin Intrigue!

Every month, you'll meet six new heroes who are guaranteed to make your spine tingle and your pulse pound. With them you'll enter into the exciting world of Harlequin Intrigue— where your life is on the line and so is your heart!

THAT'S INTRIGUE—
ROMANTIC SUSPENSE
AT ITS BEST!

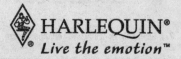

HARLEQUIN®
Live the emotion™